THE
CRYING
ROCKS

THE CRYING ROCKS

Janet Taylor Lisle

Janet Taylor Lisle

- 2007 -

Simon Pulse

NEW YORK LONDON TORONTO SYDNEY

SIMON PULSE
An imprint of Simon & Schuster Children's Publishing Division
1230 Avenue of the Americas, New York, NY 10020
Text copyright © 2003 by Janet Taylor Lisle
All rights reserved, including the right of reproduction in whole or in part in any form.
SIMON PULSE and colophon are registered trademarks of
Simon & Schuster, Inc.
Also available in an Atheneum Books for
Young Readers hardcover edition.
Designed by Polly Kanevsky
The text of this book was set in Meridien.
Manufactured in the United States of America
First Simon Pulse edition July 2005
1 2 3 4 5 6 7 8 9 10
The Library of Congress has cataloged the hardcover edition as follows:
Lisle, Janet Taylor.
The crying rocks / Janet Taylor Lisle.—1st ed.
p. cm.
"A Richard Jackson book."
Summary: Thirteen-year-old Joelle has always wondered about her life
before being adopted by the woman she calls Aunt Mary Louise and
her husband, Vernon, and she makes some surprising discoveries while
researching a seventeenth-century Indian tribe.
ISBN 0-689-85319-X (hc.)
[1. Orphans—Fiction. 2. Identity—Fiction.
3. Fathers and daughters—Fiction. 4. Indians of North America—
Rhode Island—Fiction. 5. Rhode Island—Fiction.]
I. Title.
PZ7.L6912Cr 2003
[Fic]—dc21 2002151484
ISBN 0-689-85320-3 (pbk.)

For my mother

EVERY MORNING BEFORE JOELLE COMES out of the house to go to school, there is little Misti Martin waiting for her on the sidewalk. She stands behind the low prickly hedge, dangling her lunch box in one hand and staring with worshipful eyes at Joelle's front door, whose paint is peeling off and screen is ripped.

"That China girl is out there again," Aunt Mary Louise calls, catching sight of her figure from the upstairs window. "What's she want with you, anyway, a little kid like that?"

"Nothing," Joelle yells back, "and don't bother to come down. I'm making my own breakfast."

Aunt Mary Louise hasn't been feeling up to

par since summer. First it was her back. Now her legs are giving her trouble. She used to get up at 6:00 A.M. to fix Vernon something to eat before he left for work at the turkey ranch. Lately, she's not even making it downstairs before Joelle has to leave.

The moment Joelle appears at the door, Misti's mouth drops open an inch or so. Her fine-rimmed eyes widen, as if she's seen something marvelous. Joelle strides across the beat-up lawn on her long legs and pushes through the prickly hedge, now bristling with the red berries of fall.

"How's it going, Misti?"

"Okay," she says.

"So what's for lunch today?" Joelle asks, looking down at the lunch box.

"A bologna sandwich without mustard, and a boiled egg," Misti barely breathes, collapsed with shyness.

"Well, that's a surprise," Joelle says, trying to keep things light. "That is truly a big surprise."

Misti nods. She eats the same thing for lunch every day. Seven days a week, four weeks a month, twelve months a year, a bologna sandwich without mustard, and a boiled egg. Joelle could say something mean about this if she wanted, but she holds back. Misti is too little to rag on.

"Do you have art today?" she asks instead, stooping over to speak as they begin to walk along. Misti, who is eight, is very small for her age, while Joelle, at thirteen, has grown unusually tall, five feet nine inches at last measurement and still going. There must have been a church steeple somewhere back in her family tree, Aunt Mary Louise often jokes.

"No art today," Misti answers, just above a whisper. She has coal black hair like Joelle, but shiny and sleek instead of thick. As best she can, she's wearing it the same way Joelle's wearing hers, pinned back with barrettes behind the ears.

"Oh yeah, I forgot. Only on Fridays, right? That's terrible, art just once a week. They should have it more. Especially for people like us, who really love it."

"You like it too?" Misti dares to ask. She's not really Chinese, but Japanese. Or rather, half Japanese. Aunt Mary Louise knows this, she just doesn't always remember to make the distinction. Misti's mother came from Japan when she was a child herself, and later met and married her father, who is an American. Misti was born and has lived her whole life so far just down the street.

"I used to," Joelle says, "when I was your age. I remember we made necklaces out of beer tabs one time. And another time we carved pendants out of wood. You know what a pendant is, right? It's like a charm you wear around your neck? I've still got mine somewhere. Do they let you do jewelry?"

Misti doesn't answer. She peeks up at Joelle, then glances away fast, as if she's walking with the sun or, anyway, with something too bright to look at for very long.

"Are you really a lost royal princess?" she blurts out suddenly. "Penny Perrino said you are but you don't want to tell people."

Joelle comes to a stop and looks down. "A *what*?" she explodes. "A lost *what*?"

Misti jumps.

"Listen, don't ask me that stuff," Joelle yells at her. "I don't want to hear that stuff anymore, okay?"

Misti's mouth quivers and she stares at the ground.

"I'm sorry, I didn't mean to yell." Joelle puts her arm around Misti's narrow shoulders. They start walking again. "I'm just tired of questions like that, all right? I don't even want to think about questions like that."

Misti nods sadly. Soon her sunstruck face is glancing up, though. Both of them know that tomorrow morning she'll be standing outside Joelle's house, waiting to walk with her again.

As everyone in school and many people in the small town of Marshfield, Rhode Island, are aware, Joelle is adopted. Aunt Mary Louise was open about it right from the beginning, though she needn't have said a word and anyone could have guessed. Joelle has never looked the least thing like her, or like Vernon, her adoptive father, for that matter. Where they are sandy-colored, Joelle is dark. Where they are heavy and earthbound, she is agile and quick. Joelle carries herself with a brisk aloofness that bears no resemblance to her aunt's hearty manner. Perhaps it's these differences that have inspired people to speculate about Joelle's background over the years. She's sick of it. This new rumor of royal blood is particularly crazy. Misti's friend, Penny, probably picked up a strand of gossip at school this fall. Now, in the girls' minds, and also in the minds of a number of their friends, Joelle has become something exotic and fascinating.

On her way home from school Joelle often sees this group of girls huddled across the street in front of their elementary school, watching for her. They're the walkers, the ones who live close enough so their parents don't worry about them coming and going by themselves. They're there when she walks by this afternoon, whispering frantically behind their hands.

She told me she doesn't like to talk about being a princess, Joelle imagines Misti saying. *Which must mean she is one!*

Misti must have passed along some story since this morning because everyone falls silent and follows Joelle with knowing eyes as she goes by. Joelle doesn't speak to them. She holds her head up and strides on. It's become embarrassing, this pack of little girls always on her tail. She stands out enough as it is, and not in a way that's any good to stand out.

In her own class Joelle isn't popular. There her height is a sign of weirdness. The boys are all shorter. Besides, people notice her skin. It's a dusty auburn color unlike anyone else's. The black kids know she's not one of them. She doesn't look Hispanic or Asian, either.

"Where *do* you think you're from?" someone asked her just the other day, the girl named Melinda, who wears black eyeliner and high-heeled boots to class.

"Where do you think *you're* from, *Playboy* magazine?" Joelle had fired back, loudly, so everyone would hear.

She has a talent for saying the perfect terrible thing to stop people in their tracks. To keep them away. The "in" girls avoid her like the plague. Even the older boys are wary, ever since she told Buddy Guinn, the football captain, his fly was open and he actually looked down.

"Get lost, okay?" Joelle shouts over her shoulder to Misti and her troop, who are sneaking along in her wake. She flashes around the corner and heads down the first of three long blocks toward home. There on the sidewalk ahead of her is the kid Carlos, who's in her Spanish class. You'd think with a name like Carlos he could already speak Spanish, but he can't. He's at square one, the *buenos días–muchas gracias* level, with her.

Just as she's about to catch up and pass him, he leans way over and grabs something off the ground. Then he crouches down to look at it in his hand.

Joelle doesn't especially want to talk to him, but there he is, blocking her path, so she says, "Excuse me!" in a sarcastic voice.

The kid leaps a mile and spins around. "Sorry! I didn't think anyone was behind me."

"Well, they were," Joelle says, stepping out to go around him. She tries to see what's in his hand, but he snaps his palm shut, practically on her nose.

"The crown jewels?" she asks, coming to a halt.

Carlos shakes his head, embarrassed. He has a long, thin face and, when he looks up at her, gray eyes.

"Scientific research?" Joelle suggests next. "Mutant ants? Killer worms?"

"Ha-ha," Carlos says, not laughing. He opens his hand and lets Joelle peer in.

"A stone," she says. "Brilliant."

"Not a stone, an arrowhead."

"No kidding." Joelle bends closer.

"See this edge? It's been honed."

"Honed?"

"Sharpened. It's man-made, but a long time ago. You can see the striations of a sharpening tool, most likely another rock. Indians were all around here, you know. This is Narragansett, probably."

Joelle steps away. Carlos is at least two inches shorter than she is, and his hand is muddy. She remembers him from class, one of the hyperserious morons who live in the back row.

"So what is this? You go around collecting Indian stuff? It's just lying on the ground after all these years? You can lean over and there's an arrowhead?" She looks at him skeptically.

"Yes, you can," Carlos says, staring back. "Anyone can find them. Here and in the forest." He swings his arm wide to indicate the back-roads area that starts about a mile down the main road. "I have a bunch of these. I found an ax head one time."

"An ax head. Well, no thank you," Joelle

says. "I'm not into Indians at the moment. I'm into keeping a move on so the posse doesn't catch up with me." She points over his shoulder to where a bustle of little-girl feet is just rounding the corner.

"*Hasta la vista,*" she tells Carlos, and takes off. The last she sees of him, he's turned around and is taking stock of Misti and her approaching troop, as if they're some weirdly interesting collectible phenomenon in their own right.

About Joelle's life before she was adopted, there isn't a lot known for sure.

This is probably a good thing, Aunt Mary Louise has said, since the few facts that have turned up are not exactly happy, and they point off in directions that could end up being worse. Aunt Mary Louise still gets indignant just thinking about the whole situation.

What would have happened if Joelle hadn't been rescued when she was? Where would she be now if Vernon and Aunt Mary Louise hadn't been there, practically on the spot, when she was brought in from the railway depot? A scrawny five-year-old child, abandoned by the world!

Joelle doesn't like this kind of question any more than the one Misti asked about being a princess.

"Don't ask *me*! I can't remember anything," she snaps at Aunt Mary Louise. It's the truth, she can't. Whatever happened during those first five years, there's no trace of it left in her mind. She has feelings sometimes, odd flashes of having done something or been somewhere before, but they never lead anywhere. Still, she keeps her ears open whenever the subject comes up. There's always the chance some fresh clue might surface, a fragment of a truth that she could plug into the scanty body of her larger truth.

Joelle has never told anyone this, but over the years she's woven together a story about herself based on the few facts Aunt Mary Louise has been able to supply. It's about how this little baby was born in Chicago to a mother who couldn't take care of it. She tried, for four years she tried, but she was too young, or too poor, or maybe she got sick, who knows? Whatever, she ended up penniless, on welfare, living in a series of bad apartments, and while she was in one of them her child, in a moment of senselessness, was thrown out a third-story window.

"Me?" Joelle had asked when she first heard this. "I was thrown?"

"Cast to the winds," Aunt Mary Louise declared. "What you must think of the world!"

Joelle had known right away it couldn't have happened that way. No mother on Earth would cast her child to any wind. The way Joelle imagines it, she got pushed out by accident or crawled too far over the sill. She can't prove it, though, because after the window episode, the facts in the story get even sketchier.

The mother vanishes from the scene while the child, apparently recovered from her fall, ends up in an orphanage, then disappears from Chicago altogether. Nothing more is known about her.

"So, how did I get here?" Joelle had naturally asked.

"They say you rode east on a freight train," is all Aunt Mary Louise can come up with.

"A freight train! Why?"

Aunt Mary Louise shrugs. No explanation has come to light. Was the trip a result of falling out the window? Was the child being delivered to another family? No one knows. Time has passed. Layers of other facts have settled over the first facts, sealing them off, holding them, for the moment, incommunicado.

When the child surfaces again she is living in a wooden crate near a railway depot in southern Connecticut, under the care of an elderly woman who has taught her to scavenge for half-smoked cigarettes and cigar stubs along the tracks.

"That's what you used to do for a living," Aunt Mary Louise teases Joelle whenever she tells this part of the story, which suddenly blooms with detail—whether real or an extension of Aunt Mary Louise's colorful imagination is unclear. "You'd get sent out every day to look for butts lying in the dirt. Only when you found enough—say, ten or so—were you allowed to come back and give them to the old lady. Who was a nutcake, I guess. Probably one of those loonies they let out of the state bin. Then she'd give you a piece of candy or a pack of crackers. If you didn't find any butts, I suppose you wouldn't get anything to eat."

"Well, I can't remember," Joelle replies.

"Just as well," Aunt Mary Louise says, lighting up a cigarette of her own. She's always got her pack nearby.

"I can't remember being born in Chicago, or falling out the window, or riding the freight train, either," Joelle announces. "You keep saying I did all that, but how do I know?"

"Oh, you did it all right." Aunt Mary Louise nods. "Family Services checked up on you before the papers got signed. They said we should know what we were letting ourselves in for."

This is another joke Aunt Mary Louise likes to tell, the "what we were letting ourselves in for" joke. And Joelle had always allowed it to go by. She hadn't liked it, but she let it go, until last week when hearing it one more time, she'd surprised herself by getting furious.

"You made that up!" she'd yelled at Aunt Mary Louise. "Family Services never would've said that. It's too mean to the little child. Anyway, I wasn't the only one they had to check out before the papers got signed. They checked out you and Vernon, too. They don't just hand kids over like a fruit basket, you know!"

Aunt Mary Louise was astonished.

"Sweetie, don't get so upset. Of course they checked us out," she'd answered, tapping her cigarette in midair by mistake and dripping ashes down the front of her sweater.

For some reason, this had made Joelle even madder.

"Why don't you quit that smoking?" she'd yelled at her. "It's making you sick. Sick!" She'd run into her room and slammed the door.

But later she'd come out and put her arms around Aunt Mary Louise's neck and hugged her.

"I guess I was more upset than I thought," she whispered.

"I shouldn't wonder," Aunt Mary Louise said, "after all you've been through." She forgave her and hugged her back.

"And don't you worry, there's nothing wrong with me," she'd told Joelle. "I'm just tired, sweetie. I'm taking a little rest. I'll be back to my old self in no time, you'll see."

TWO DAYS AFTER THE "LOST PRINCESS"
question Misti comes up with another crazy
remark. She and Joelle are on their walk to
school. Joelle has gone through the "what's
for lunch?" routine and a few others when
Misti suddenly turns to her and whispers:
"You have a secret admirer!"

"A what?" Joelle snaps. "What are you
talking about?"

"Look," Misti says. She points shyly with
her lunch box, and there is Carlos saunter-
ing up a side street, still some distance off.
"He follows us every day."

This is so absurd that Joelle laughs. "Of
course he follows us. It's how he walks to

school. He lives down there somewhere, in the woods."

Misti says nothing more. She closes her mouth and looks smugly at the sidewalk.

"Why do you think he's following *me*?" Joelle asks. "Maybe he's following *you*." Over her shoulder, she sees that Carlos now is, in fact, behind them, plodding along. His serious face is looking down, as if he's hunting for arrowheads again.

Misti sneaks another peek. She giggles and begins slamming her lunch box into the side of her leg.

"What's so funny?" Joelle demands.

Misti shrugs. If she knows something, she's not telling. A minute later she spots one of her little buddies and runs off toward the elementary school, not even saying good-bye.

Joelle enters her own school at top speed and without looking back again. When Spanish class comes up, she gets there early and sits in the front row, where she stares at the blackboard while everyone else straggles in around her. She doesn't look behind, but she feels that Carlos is there. Her back begins to prickle, as if his eyes had spikes in them.

This is stupid. It's so stupid that she finally turns all the way around and stares angrily at the place where he usually sits.

He's there, all right—slouched down, writing in a notebook and not noticing her a bit. Whatever Misti thinks she knows is completely wrong. Joelle suspected it all along. She turns back, Spanish class begins, and that's it. She dismisses Carlos from her mind. Well, sort of.

A few days later she happens to run into him again. She's out doing a grocery errand for Aunt Mary Louise in the late afternoon and has taken a back route through the scruffy town park. This is to throw Misti and her bloodhounds off her scent. Lately, they've taken to following her back to her house after school and hanging around outside the hedge. The one called Penny is older—she's actually in third grade, not second—and the real ringleader. She dares the others to do things—touch the front porch, knock on the door—and then acts disgusted when they won't. When someone tells her to do it herself, she says she can't because she asked them first. From her

upstairs bedroom, Joelle can hear everything.

Carlos is over on one side of the park, the
really overgrown side near the swamp. He's
alone, except for a dark, lumpish figure
seated at the old barbecue pit across the way.
This is Queenie, the town vagrant and free
spirit, who camps out there whenever she
can get away with it. Her ancient red VW
Bug is parked nearby, stuffed with newspapers and old clothes. Out of habit, Joelle
gives her a wide berth. She could avoid
Carlos, too, but at the last minute she veers
over to him.

"*Buenos días, amigo!* What are you looking
for now?" she asks in a loud voice.

He whirls around like the last time.

"*Buenos días,*" he echoes. After this a
silence develops while he shifts his weight
nervously. He's worse in English than Spanish, it seems. Generously, Joelle decides to
help him out.

"So tell me about these Indians who were
supposedly around here," she says, as if
she's never heard of Indians before. Which
is laughable. Half the names of places in
Rhode Island are Native American. There

are statues of Indians in the parks and plaques that tell where this treaty was signed or that attack happened. Everyone has heard of the Indians, they just don't think about them that much. Indians are ancient history here, like three hundred years ago or more.

"Narragansetts," Carlos says, bending down again, possibly to avoid looking at her. "They're interesting."

"Why?" Joelle asks. "Nobody's left, are they?"

"Nobody from those times, but their artifacts are still around."

"Arrowheads," Joelle says. "Sounds like constant warfare back then."

"They used them to hunt, too."

"I guess they had to eat."

"In terms of war, it wasn't that bad, actually," Carlos says, warming up a little. "The Narragansetts were a great people. They were the largest tribe in New England, but they used their power to keep peace. Back in the woods there's a place where they used to meet. A high council place. There are trails, too. You can tell they're old Indian paths because of how deep they're worn down. It would take hundreds of years of feet to wear down a path like that."

Carlos looks to see what Joelle makes of this.

"Hundreds of years of *feet*?" she says. "Give me a break."

"A thousand years, even. Some artifacts are that old and more. What's amazing is how their whole culture got wiped out when the white man came. Fifty years after the Pilgrims landed at Plymouth Rock, the Narragansetts were all gone, thirty or forty thousand people who lived right around here."

"What happened?" Joelle asks, in spite of herself.

Carlos stares at her. "Disease, first, then they were killed off. The last few were sold into slavery down in the West Indies. It's one of those histories people don't like to remember."

"But you do?"

"I'm part Indian."

"Really?"

Carlos stands up straighter and looks at her defiantly, as if she might have a problem with this. She registers again his gray eyes, his brown hair, his long, thin face.

"You don't look—"

"Just a small part," Carlos says quickly. "Like about one-sixteenth or something. My grandmother never told anybody, but after she died, my father found out from an old birth certificate that her father was part Sioux. From out West, not around here. Like I said, mostly everybody here got wiped out."

Suddenly Joelle feels out of her depth. Maybe Carlos's long root of identity is too much to handle. Also, he's talking easily now, acting too friendly. Another minute and he might start asking her about herself.

"Well, I have to go," she says, moving off. "I'm on a top secret mission, one step ahead of the law."

"Somebody's on your tail again?" Carlos asks, glancing around. He examines the hunched form of Queenie at the barbecue pit with complete seriousness.

"I was kidding!"

"Oh." He looks deflated. "Bye," he calls, looking after her. He bends down to start Indian artifact hunting again, then abruptly stands.

"If you ever want to see the council place, let

me know. I can show you where it is," he calls.

Joelle doesn't answer. She's walking away fast, not about to be lured back into conversation. Carlos tries again:

"Hey! You know, you kind of look like them."

"Who?" she yells over her shoulder.

"The Narragansetts," Carlos yells. "Check it out in the library. There's a painting."

This is so clearly a last desperate effort for attention that Joelle laughs. She is now sprinting, past Queenie's red Bug (she sees the old woman's sharp eyes watch her go by), along the road, toward the grocery store. She pulls out Aunt Mary Louise's grocery list and reads it, between jogs, to get herself back on course.

Hamburger, milk, frozen peas, paper towels. This guy Carlos is a total fruitcake. You could be one-sixteenth anything, raccoon or great white whale, and it wouldn't mean a thing, she thinks. By one-sixteenth there's almost nothing left of the original. One-sixteenth drop of blood in water probably wouldn't even show up.

"I could be one-sixteenth lost royal princess, for Pete's sake!" Joelle calls angrily to the passing traffic as she runs. "Wait till Misti hears that! She'll go bananas!"

Joelle has been with Vernon and Aunt Mary Louise for as long as she can remember, which is more than eight years now, she's been told. From time to time, she's tried to imagine what it must have been like to live in a wooden crate.

She's looked back in her memory and tried to see the kind of crate it might have been. Was it like the big wooden packing case Vernon brought back from the dump to use for storing fertilizer? Or was it smaller, like the cardboard box the new washing machine came in? Their old washer overflowed for the last time and was kicked out the kitchen door. Things that break down get on Vernon's nerves. He's not a fixer, Aunt Mary Louise has explained. Some men are and some aren't, she said, contrary to public notion.

In her mind Joelle has placed the crate, at times one kind, at times another, beside some tracks near a busy train station. The story goes that the crate was located "near a depot," which is a kind of small freight station, according to Aunt Mary Louise. She isn't Joelle's real aunt, of course. Joelle has no aunts that anyone knows of. She has no uncles or cousins or grandparents, either. She was a lost child. Lost and found by the railroad tracks and then rescued by Vernon and Aunt Mary Louise at the Family Services Center in Badgerville, Connecticut.

"Can I see it sometime?"

"What, Family Services? There's nothing to see. It was an office."

"So who found me first?"

"The police, I suppose."

"At the railway depot?"

"One day in late September. It was getting cool."

"What was the old lady's name who had me?"

"No word on that. She probably didn't know herself. Imagine keeping a small child in a box!"

"Was there a bed in the box? Did I sleep there at night?"

Joelle used to ask such things, back when

she was still dumb enough to think they were important.

"A bed!" Aunt Mary Louise snorted the way she does whenever something is completely the opposite of what someone thinks. Her cheeks quivered. She's older than other kids' mothers. Her hair is gray and her legs are fat. Nests of wormy blue veins bulge out behind her knees.

"You slept on a pile of greasy rags that wasn't fit for rats, let alone you," she told Joelle one time. "And dirt? Whew! The Family Services woman said you were the grimiest little child they ever picked up. You hadn't had a bath for a year. Can you imagine that? A year!"

Recently, Joelle has quit asking direct questions about her past. She figures she has more than enough information already. She has eight years' worth of information, assuming that Aunt Mary Louise is right about when she was adopted. She's not always exact about facts, Joelle has noticed. This depot Joelle was found in, for instance—sometimes she says it's outside New Haven and sometimes up near Hartford. Vernon could probably clear this up, but he isn't a talker and doesn't like questions.

It's annoying enough to be told the same story over and over. What's worse is when you can't depend on the story being right. It's happened a hundred times that just as Joelle begins to feel comfortable about her facts, Aunt Mary Louise will change something. She'll come out with some new detail that messes everything up.

The pile of greasy rags is a good example. Before Aunt Mary Louise told her about it, Joelle had imagined the crate by the railway depot as being kind of an interesting place. It had a clean wooden floor and a sleeping bag, or at least a few blankets folded in a corner. When she finished looking for cigarette butts, the small child who was Joelle would snuggle down into the sleeping bag. She would look out the door of the box house at the lights of the trains that rumbled by at night. She would nibble on some crackers she kept hidden in a secret hole, and the way Joelle imagined it, she wouldn't feel too bad.

Aunt Mary Louise's sudden addition of the greasy rags upset this notion. They were so disgusting. The mention of rats made Joelle's skin crawl. She stopped thinking about the box and started concentrating on what might have been happening outside in the railway depot. It wasn't easy at first. What did she know about train stations? They went everywhere by car. The only station she'd been in was for the bus one time, to go to Providence, when Vernon's truck broke down. Then, it seemed she did know things. Her mind loosened up.

Trains rumbled into the depot. People waiting there hugged one another good-bye, then bent to pick up their suitcases. Engines screeched to a stop, blowing out humid air. The old woman who kept Joelle in the box was impressed by the number of butts Joelle found every day. One time the woman handed over a whole Snickers bar for a reward. A homeless dog came up and watched while Joelle ate it. She shared the last bite with the dog, and they became friends.

After this, in her imagination, Joelle always had the dog with her when she went out butt hunting. What was her name? Silver Girl or something like that. The dog slept with her at night, too, came inside the box with her because she was a small dog and afraid to be alone.

"Don't worry, I'll take care of you. Stay with me. We'll be safe," Joelle told her.

The pile of rags was still there, somewhere, but the memory of sleeping with that dog, close up against her hot, furry side, spread over it. Gradually, the rags shrank in importance. The rats disappeared. Joelle took the box back, away from them, and made it the way she wanted.

3

A FEW DAYS LATER, AFTER SCHOOL,
Joelle drops by the public library. She has a
report to do on the history of the vanilla
bean. Don't ask why. It's for science. Everybody in class has been assigned an herb or a
spice. They've been told to research its Latin
name, locate the country of origin, trace the
trade routes by which said herb or spice was
introduced around the world. Joelle was
handed vanilla by pure chance. She doesn't
even like it, never orders vanilla ice cream
(too boring) and doesn't bother adding the
one teaspoon or whatever that the brownie
mix calls for. Nobody knows the difference
whether it's there or not.

It's while she is trying to copy, freehand from
a book, an illustration of a vanilla bean living

in the wild—a wild vanilla bean, no less—that she remembers what Carlos said in the park a few days before. A painting at the library. Of Narragansett Indians that supposedly look like her. Which can't be right because, from everything she's heard, Native Americans were short. On TV they look compact, thick-necked, muscular, the exact opposite of her. Admittedly, this image comes mostly from old Hollywood movies, but scriptwriters do research, don't they? They consult old photos?

Anyway, it's time for a break, so she gets up from her worktable, stretches, and takes a stroll around.

She finds the painting almost immediately: a long mural, dark with age, spread across the back wall between the bathrooms. It's composed of stiffly painted Native American figures busy with various conventional occupations: weaving baskets, harvesting corn, fishing, offering a visiting white man something . . . tobacco leaves? Well, there's a disease bomb waiting to explode.

Other scenes include Indian children playing with a dog—did Indians even have dogs back then?—and a woman carrying a papoose on her back. From the forest's leafy gloom, a group of Indian men is just returning from a hunt with a couple of dead deer slung on their backs. Balancing this scene, four smiling Pilgrim fathers are striding up another path, holding a document that probably has to do with land sales. As everybody knows, Native Americans were tricked by the white man into giving up their territory.

She yawns. The whole mural is a cliché, something out of a textbook. There's nothing real about it, and certainly no one who looks like her. Except . . . She steps closer.

In the mural's dark background, off to one side where she missed her at first, she sees an Indian girl standing straight and tall as a young tree. Her black hair is plaited in two thick braids that fall below her shoulders. She is holding the hand of another, smaller girl, also wearing braids, half hidden by bushes. With grave expressions, the two are watching the bustling village scene before them, their faces so alike they could be sisters.

Joelle takes a step closer and stares up. A spark of recognition flashes inside her. There's something about the two figures she seems to recall. It doesn't last. Even as she gazes, the figures flatten, become a painted abstraction. Joelle retreats a few steps, looks up again. The girls' identical faces reform, then *flash!* That spark again.

What is going on?

Whatever it is, Joelle doesn't like it. A shadowy memory is moving inside her, coming up from some place she never knew existed and doesn't want to investigate. Time to leave. Yes, it's late. She should be getting home for supper.

She turns away and walks fast back to her table. She slips the vanilla bean drawing into a notebook, loads her backpack, and slings it over a shoulder. A minute later she is outside in the crisp October air, striding on her long legs down the sidewalk, leaving the library and its stereotypical Indian scene in the dust. Never has she seen such a fake and stupid painting. There should be a law against allowing dumb pictures like that in a public place, she tells herself.

It's after 5:30 P.M. when Joelle gets home, and she can see Vernon's pickup sitting in the driveway. He's a manager at the big turkey ranch outside of town, in charge of feeding and watering and raking up droppings under the flocks, which live in uncomfortable-looking wire cages hung high over the ground. He puts in a long day, but he's always back by 5:30 P.M. If he wants to go out, he goes out later, after supper, which is nice of him, respectful of the trouble Aunt Mary Louise goes to to make his dinner every night.

Nearing the house, however, Joelle hears angry voices. In recent months some bone of contention has risen between them. What it might be, she can't guess because they never argue main issues. They wrangle over small things that rub them the wrong way.

"Shut up yourself and take off those boots before you go in my kitchen!" she hears Aunt Mary Louise yell.

"Get off my back!" Vernon shouts. "You've always got some complaint."

"You bring the whole turkey ranch back here with you every day. Whew! What a stink! It's making me sick."

"You're always sick. I'm sick of you being sick!"

The minute Joelle comes in, they stop.

Vernon goes out the back door into the yard with a hangdog look. Aunt Mary Louise tries to smile and asks her how her day went. She doesn't listen to Joelle's answer, though. She's too steamed up to concentrate.

"I'm sorry, sweetie. We're not really that mad at each other," she says, doing her best to smooth things over.

She goes and lies down on the couch, then asks Joelle if she'll set the table and finish cutting up the green beans for supper, to give her time to get her wits back. Luckily, the rest is cooked and ready—fried chicken, potato salad—because Vernon might get worked up all over again if they don't eat by six.

Not that he'd normally get worked up about something dumb like that. He's quiet most of the time, soft-spoken and polite. It's just that when he's already in a bad mood, the Irish in him comes out. Then everyone has to tiptoe around. Once he threw an iron frying pan out the kitchen window into the backyard. The window was open but there was a screen in it, and the frying pan sailed right through the screen with no trouble at all.

"You see that high color Vernon's got? The

blood of the Irish runs closer to the surface than in other people, so it comes to a boil quicker," Aunt Mary Louise told Joelle one time when she was little.

This was an old wives' tale, of course, but at the time Joelle was stupid enough to believe it. She'd kept a close watch on Vernon's color after that. If he looked red, even if it was just from being out in the sun, she'd get nervous. Boiling blood came to be something she worried about. That a human body could explode from getting angry became a scientific fact in her mind, right up there with nuclear bombs and water freezing into ice.

It was a few years before she saw through to the truth. Now she has more reliable predictors of Vernon's temper. For instance, when he stops moving, just suddenly stops dead in his tracks and stares at you—when he does that, watch out.

After supper Vernon gets in the truck and leaves. Aunt Mary Louise goes back to the couch, and Joelle washes up at the sink.

"Are you feeling tired again?" she asks over the running water. She doesn't have to raise her voice to be heard since the living room is just through the door of the kitchen. Everything is close together in the house because it's so small. The ceilings are low. The rooms are stuffed with furniture. Maybe it's her recent growth spurt—she's now a full five inches taller than Aunt Mary Louise!—but lately, Joelle has begun to feel cramped in this place, like a dinosaur in a dollhouse.

Aunt Mary Louise sighs. "Seems like I don't have energy for anything these days."

"You should get out more," Joelle says over her shoulder. "You need exercise and to quit sitting around."

"I guess I do," Aunt Mary Louise agrees.

Until a year ago Aunt Mary Louise went to work along with Vernon. She did a day shift at the chicken-packaging plant south of town, which meant no one was home when Joelle got back from school. She'd open a bag of chips, get a can of soda from the fridge, and have the place to herself for a couple of hours. She'd settle down on the couch and do her homework, slowly and neatly, from beginning to end, with no interruptions. Embarrassing to admit, but she likes doing homework. She enjoys memorizing history dates and making math problems come out right. Tests aren't that hard for her. Somehow she always knows the answers. She actually feels steadier, more orderly when she's taking them, though she keeps this to herself. It's just another weird thing about her for people at school to fasten on.

Unfortunately, Aunt Mary Louise lost her chicken plant job. She was laid off because her legs started hurting and she couldn't stand up all day and gut chickens. She put in for a sit-down position, but never heard if she was even in the running. Now, whenever Joelle gets home from school, she's there, lying on the couch, smoking the place up and reading a novel. She keeps stacks of them on the floor of her closet, worn-out paperbacks she picks up at yard sales with titles like *Dark Side of Desire* and *Jailbirds Don't Sing*.

"I'm serious. You have to take better care of your health," Joelle says, sitting down beside her after the dishes are finished.

"I know," Aunt Mary Louise murmurs. You can see she's not about to change anything.

"Are there any Indians that you heard about in my background?" Joelle asks her suddenly.

"Indians? You mean like warpath Indians?"

"Yes."

"Uh-uh. Not that I was ever told," Aunt Mary Louise says. "You came from Chicago."

"I know."

"On a freight train, they said."

"I know that. I just wondered if—"

"Which always seemed strange to me. I mean, why a freight train? Why didn't you come on a regular passenger train or by bus like everyone else?"

"How do I know?"

"Did I ever tell you about that first day you came to live with us?"

"You did."

"About what you said when we brought you into your room here for the first time and showed you your bed?"

"I heard," Joelle says more loudly, but Aunt Mary Louise doesn't register. She is bright-eyed and far away.

"Me and Vernon had you by the hand, one on each side, and we brought you into your room, which we'd got all fixed up for your arrival, and you said, 'Do I get my own pillow?'"

Joelle doesn't say anything. She focuses

her eyes on the floor and keeps them there.

"Remember? It was so cute. 'Do I get my own pillow?' you asked, in this teeny-weeny voice. Because you'd always had to share it, I guess, like with your crazy mother who threw you out the window. Or maybe you just never had a pillow at all. Can you imagine that? A child who never had a pillow to lay her head on?"

"You told me that before."

"I guess I have," Aunt Mary Louise says.

"About a hundred times."

"You should tell me to shut up."

Joelle looks at her. She feels helpless, as if she's caught in a net. Half of her is angry, furious even, that Aunt Mary Louise would tell her this, over and over, without thinking how it might make her feel. There's no more pathetic thing than a little child asking, "Do I get my own pillow?" as if she'd never been anything to anybody her whole life, as if she were a throw-out. Who needs to be reminded of that?

But the other half of Joelle knows that Aunt Mary Louise is telling her this story because she loves her. It's one of the precious memories that Aunt Mary Louise hoards, that she brings out to make herself feel better. Because things in Aunt Mary Louise's life haven't always been so great. And they especially aren't great right now.

"So nothing about Indians that you can remember?"

Aunt Mary Louise shakes her head.

"Somebody said I looked like one."

"An *Indian*?" Aunt Mary Louise snorts. "You've got South America in you, that's what I think. Vernon said something about the West Indies one time. He did some research on you but never found out much. How you made it up to Chicago to get yourself born, I don't know."

"Someday I'm going to that office in Badgerville and check things out for myself," Joelle says, standing up.

"You won't find anything there. That office was closed. I know because I wanted medical information about you a few years ago and there was no sign of the place. Then I heard you could contact a state agency in Hartford, but when I called up there, you weren't in the records."

"There must be information written down

somewhere. Maybe they didn't want to tell you. They could have been trying to protect people who didn't want me to find out about them."

"Maybe." Aunt Mary Louise heaves a distracted sigh. Her hand finds its way to the cigarette pack on the coffee table. "There was a bunch of Indians living down around Westerly that Vernon used to know when he worked for the railroad," she muses. "They'd all drive up to the ball games in Pawtucket on weekends."

"Hmm." Joelle glances at her watch.

"And then there's Queenie."

"That old black lady in the park? She's Indian?"

"There's a mix there, I'd guess. People say she's a descendant of one of the early tribes around here. She can't live indoors, that's one thing."

"When's Vernon getting back?" Joelle asks.

"No telling. There's no telling with him lately."

"Well, I've got homework."

"You go on, sweetie." Aunt Mary Louise glances up fondly. "Don't worry about me.

I'm just going to lie here and rest my bones. I'll be tip-top by tomorrow."

———————————

Carlos, coming face-to-face with Joelle in the hall the next day, says: "*Buenos días*. Have you been over to look in the library yet?"

"No!" Joelle says.

Carlos drops his eyes and gets ready to go on by, but then Joelle changes her mind and says, "Okay, yeah, I went."

"You did?"

"The Narragansetts don't look like me."

"Not exactly, I know, but——"

"They're shrimps, for one thing."

"Oh," says Carlos. "I just thought there was something about——"

"And they're not even real!" Joelle adds in disgust. "The artist didn't care what anyone looked like, he was just painting types. Black hair, beads, peace pipes. They could be anyone. You're the Indian around here. . . . Do they look like you?"

"No," Carlos says quietly.

"Do I look like a type?"

"No."

"I was born in Chicago!" Joelle shouts angrily. "I don't even come from around here!"

She glances away. She's never told anyone any of her facts. Here she is sounding off in a public hallway. She steals a look at Carlos, who appears to be suffering under her barrage.

"Sorry," he mutters.

"It's okay, don't worry about it. People always get me wrong. I'm not what anybody thinks."

Carlos nods without looking. He really isn't that much shorter than she is, Joelle notices. He must have been standing on low ground before. She likes the way he doesn't try to defend himself by getting angry back.

"I was thinking about that Indian council place," she finds herself announcing a second later. "You know, the place in the woods you were talking about?"

"You want to go?" Carlos gazes at her in surprise.

"No. But I might change my mind."

"We could go tomorrow. This afternoon

I'm driving with my mother to pick up my father at the airport in Providence."

"Where's your father been?"

"To California, for a medical conference. He's an orthopedist."

"A what?"

"He specializes in bones."

"Big deal."

Carlos nods thoughtfully, as if he's really considering this. "How about if I meet you outside school tomorrow?" he goes on.

"In back," Joelle says. "The posse is out front."

"Oh, right." Faint lines of what may actually be a smile appear on Carlos's long face. "Why are they after you, anyway?"

"Because I'm royal."

"What?"

"And lost."

"Huh?"

"They want to rescue me."

"From who?"

"I'm kidding."

"Cariño mio!" exclaims Carlos. "When will I learn?"

They walk in opposite directions down the hall.

4

THE MINUTE JOELLE GETS HOME FROM
school that afternoon, she goes to her room
and gets out the thick Spanish-English dictionary she uses to do her Spanish homework. She bought it cheap from an older girl
who dropped the course over the summer.

Sitting on her bed, Joelle thumbs through
for the word *cariño* and finds the translation:
"darling." She already knows that *mio* is the
word for the possessive "my." So, unless she's
totally crazy, *cariño mio* translates as "my
darling."

But would Carlos ever knowingly say such
a thing? Never. He'd die of embarrassment if
he knew. He was just repeating a phrase
Mrs. Correja, their Spanish teacher, blurts
out from time to time, usually when some-

one has made a specially horrible mistake in pronunciation. Cariño mio, *your brain is thick as mud!* is what she means, though she never completes her sentence. Carlos probably thought she was swearing.

Still, just thinking that he said something like that to her makes Joelle blush. He is such a weirdo. Why a person would want to hike to some dumb Indian council place way off in the woods, alone with him, she doesn't know. She should call him right now and say she can't go after all.

"I'll be a little late getting home tomorrow," she ends up telling Aunt Mary Louise later, in the kitchen. They're together at the counter, peeling carrots and chopping them into pieces for dinner. Aunt Mary Louise has offered to make glazed carrots with butter and brown sugar, a special treat that Vernon loves.

"I have to do a project on Indians with some other kids. We're walking to a ceremonial meeting place in the woods."

"That's nice," Aunt Mary Louise says, bending over to look in the fridge.

"This whole area was full of Narragansett Indians at one time. Their artifacts are still around," Joelle informs her, exercising Carlos's word. It sounds so professional.

"Artifacts, hmm," says Aunt Mary Louise.

"You know what those are, right?" Joelle asks.

Aunt Mary Louise went to school only through the ninth grade. Though she's a reader, there are spaces in her knowledge of the world that Joelle has recently begun to detect.

"I know," Aunt Mary Louise says. "Bones, right?"

"They could be other things, too, like arrowheads or ax heads. You can tell when you find an arrowhead because you see striations in the stone."

"See what?" Aunt Mary Louise gazes at her.

"Striations," Joelle says. "Marks that show the stone was honed to make a sharp edge, probably with another stone."

"Oh." Aunt Mary Louise lowers her head.

"I wasn't sure what it meant either," Joelle says quickly, so she won't feel bad. "A kid I know said it, and I checked it in the dictionary to be sure I had it right."

"I should do that more," Aunt Mary

Louise answers with a weary sigh. "I never look up anything. That's why I don't know much."

"You know a lot!" Joelle protests, shocked that she'd say that. Even if it is a little true, it's nothing she can help. She had to drop out of school. Her father fell off a ladder and broke his back when she was fifteen. He couldn't work afterward, and there were five children to feed. Aunt Mary Louise was the oldest, so she applied for her father's old job in a typewriter factory in Providence. Amazingly, she was hired! (She lied about her age.) It's a story she's told many times.

Aunt Mary Louise shakes her head, then pats Joelle on her arm.

"You do it for me," she says. "Keep looking things up and being smart. That's why I went and found you, to carry on where I got stopped. I knew you had it in you when I first saw your face. Did I ever tell you about that?"

Joelle doesn't say anything. She picks another carrot out of the plastic bag and starts peeling it, though there are more than enough already.

"I recall that day so well," Aunt Mary Louise goes on eagerly. "I recall it like yesterday."

———————

The reason Aunt Mary Louise decided to adopt Joelle was that she got married to Vernon but was too old to have a real baby. They were late bloomers, past forty. One day it hit her that she had to have somebody to come after her. She couldn't just die and leave nothing behind.

"There needs to be someone who has the print of you in them, or life doesn't make sense," she's told Joelle many times.

Vernon was against the idea at first. He'd been married once before and had a child who died or something. He wasn't eager to get into that again.

Aunt Mary Louise talked and talked about a child, though. She went on for a year or more, wouldn't stop talking about it. Maybe she drove Vernon crazy because one day, suddenly, he up and agreed. He made a few phone calls, they got in the car and took a ride to Connecticut, to the center in Badgerville.

And who should be waiting there, just arrived the week before from the crate at the depot, but Joelle.

"You were not the most awe-inspiring sight in the world," Aunt Mary Louise informs her now, laying herself back heavily on the couch, going into a story Joelle has heard before, though not so often as some others. Aunt Mary Louise likes the high drama of the early stories better: crazy mothers, open windows, freight trains.

"You had nothing, just the clothes on your back when you arrived. Even after they'd cleaned you up, you didn't look too good. I remember how they brought you in and we just knew, Vernon and me, that nobody else was probably going to take you. The surface didn't look too promising. Most people who adopt want a newborn that hasn't got much experience of the world. They don't want to take a risk on the older kids, in case something has happened that's already messed them up. You can't always tell by looking at the surface. Only years later, it shows up when they start acting bad.

"Well, with you, your surface already looked bad because of you living out in the depot for who knows how long, but we could tell you were all right inside. You had good eyes that looked right at us, real sharp and curious. You didn't say anything, but you didn't cry, either. That was good because the one thing Vernon didn't want was a crybaby."

Joelle finds herself nodding. It's pathetic, but she nods, as if she wants to hear more. And the terrible thing is, she does. But she also hates listening. She hates how it makes her feel.

"And you never did cry," Aunt Mary Louise adds thoughtfully, as she has on other occasions. "Right up to now. Not when you fell or hurt yourself or were frightened. Not for anything. Why is that?"

She looks at Joelle with real curiosity. Joelle gives her a level gaze back.

"I don't know."

"Well, it's odd."

"No, it's not. Why should I cry if I don't feel like it?"

Aunt Mary Louise sighs. "I guess you shouldn't." She goes on: "Anyway, it wasn't ten minutes after they brought you in to us that I said to Vernon, 'Okay, this is the one.' And he said, 'Good choice.'"

"He did?" Joelle asks. This is new information. "You never told me he said that."

"He did."

"I thought he didn't care one way or the other. You said that before."

"Of course he cared when he saw you! He had to see you first, then his heart went out."

Joelle takes a peek at Aunt Mary Louise to be sure she's not making this up. Vernon doesn't usually let his heart go out to anything.

"So I asked the woman to tell us your name. Well, she looked at Vernon, and Vernon looked at her, and nobody knew, if you can believe it. You were so new at that place they hadn't had time to get the details yet, the few details there were. And, of course, you wouldn't say anything."

"Wait a minute," Joelle can't help breaking in. "I'd been there a week, and they hadn't given me a name in all that time?"

"I guess not," Aunt Mary Louise says, "because you didn't have one."

"That does not make sense. They would have thought one up by then."

"Well, they hadn't," Aunt Mary Louise says. "Or they hadn't wanted to call you anything until they knew the right name. Anyway, what happened was, the woman announced how she'd seen this movie on TV the night before. And—I'll never forget this—she said it was about an orphan girl named Joelle who grew up to be Miss America. I can't remember exactly what she grew up to be, but it was somebody like that. So she asked us, how would we like that name for the time being? Until they could find out what your real name was. We said that would be all right, and she wrote it down on her paper. Later, when we went to adopt you properly, they told us you'd been called Sissie in Chicago. Short for Sylvia, I think. Anyway, Vernon said you were Joelle to him by then, and he wouldn't think of changing. Vernon, is that you?"

It is Vernon, coming through the door. Early.

Aunt Mary Louise looks startled for a moment. Then she remembers what he said at dinner the night before: He had to take off from work at three o'clock today to get a tooth pulled. It was giving him trouble.

"Oh yes, I forgot," she answers, even though Vernon hasn't said anything. "That didn't take long. I guess it wasn't too bad?"

Vernon doesn't answer. His mouth looks swollen on one side. He stands inside the closed front door staring at Aunt Mary Louise in a way that makes Joelle nervous.

"Hey, Vernon, I was telling Joelle about the day we found her at that center in Badgerville, and I couldn't remember. Wasn't she named Sylvia but called Sissie when she was living out in Chicago?"

A muscle moves in Vernon's cheek.

"Well, it was something like that," Aunt Mary Louise says, turning back. "I think my memory's going to pot along with everything else. Anyway, I guess it doesn't matter what somebody calls you that throws you out a third-story window. Probably, they forgot to call you any name."

"Don't ask me, I can't remember anything," Joelle says quickly. She's seen Vernon's eyes shift. He's never liked Aunt Mary Louise telling these stories about her. Maybe it's Aunt Mary Louise's jokey approach, which can seem a little mean sometimes, or maybe he just doesn't want Joelle hearing about her life back then.

Whichever, Aunt Mary Louise is usually careful not to say too much when he's around. This time she seems almost to be challenging him.

Vernon's gaze avoids Aunt Mary Louise, propped up like a sack of flour on the couch pillows, and fixes on an unlit lamp on a table behind her. There's a long pause during which nobody moves. Or breathes, it seems. Joelle gets so nervous, she feels like screaming.

Suddenly, Vernon turns and walks straight toward her. He looks furious, as if he's about to grab her. Joelle lurches away and starts to duck, but he brushes past and goes on into the kitchen. He opens the fridge, takes out a beer, slams the fridge door shut, and disappears out the back. Joelle's face feels sweaty. She goes to sit by Aunt Mary Louise, nestles in close to her on the couch.

"Listen, don't tell those stories about me when he's around. It makes him mad," she whispers. "I thought for a minute . . ."

Aunt Mary Louise purses her lips. "He would never hurt you," she says. "Never."

"Well, don't tell them to him anyway."

Through the window, they watch Vernon stalk across the muddy yard. There's still an hour until suppertime. He's probably going to work on his shed. He has a plan to raise chicks from the egg and sell them to a local farmer to grow into chickens for the packaging plant. He knows someone who's doing that and making good money.

"And don't tell them to me, either," Joelle says to Aunt Mary Louise, loud and clear, for the first time ever. She turns to face her. "I don't want to hear them anymore. Sissie or Sylvia, I don't need to know."

Aunt Mary Louise turns her head away, as if she's insulted.

"See, it's all a big fairy tale, as far as I'm concerned. Maybe it's true and maybe it isn't. How do I know?"

"Some fairy tale; it makes me sick," Aunt Mary Louise says to the wall. "An innocent child. A little innocent girl that's abandoned by the world, left to sleep in a box. . . ." Before she can get any further, Joelle leans over and takes one of her hands. She holds it tight between her own.

"Listen, I don't care," she says quietly. "It's not a problem for me. I know it must seem like I could never forget, but I have. You shouldn't worry anymore. I can't even remember getting thrown."

5

CARLOS IS SITTING ON THE BACK STEPS
staring bleakly at the school parking lot
when Joelle comes out the door to meet him
the next afternoon. It occurs to her that he
thought she wouldn't come.

"*Ciao!*" she sings out.

He turns around quickly. "What is 'chow'?"
he asks. He's always so serious about everything.

"It's Italian for 'hi.'"

"Italian! What happened to Spanish?"

"It's boring to speak the same language all
the time. We should broaden our minds.
Sawahdee ka."

"*Sa*—what?"

"It's Thai, the language of Thailand, for

'hello.' But if you're a guy, you say *sawahdee krap.*"

"Ha-ha," says Carlos.

"You do! It's not what it sounds like. In Thailand the end of some words depends on whether the person speaking is a man or a woman. Women say *ka;* men say *krap.* I was wondering last night if that's somehow sexual discrimination. I couldn't decide. What do you think?"

Carlos has been silenced. He stares at her as if she's some bewildering form of alien intelligence, then gets up and starts walking away. Joelle follows.

"And then there's *nee-how.* That's 'hi' in Chinese," she can't stop herself from adding.

They make their way across the parking lot toward a side street, being careful to avoid the front of the school, where Misti and company lie in wait.

"Where did you learn all that?" Carlos asks as they reach the street.

"I looked it up. We had this assignment to research vanilla, and it sort of took me over to the other side of the world. Vanilla grows in Central America but also in parts of

Indonesia, I found out. After that, I don't know, I couldn't stop. I started going up into Thailand and China."

Glancing over, Joelle sees that Carlos appears really worried now, as if he might not know where Indonesia even is, not to mention Thailand. Okay, enough is enough.

"So where are we going?" she asks him, to put him in charge again. When you look too smart, ask a question. Every girl knows this.

"Up Buck Pond Road a way, then into the woods by the old quarry," he answers in a relieved voice. "There's a hiking trail there that leads along the side of the swamp. We branch off on another trail after a couple of miles and start going uphill. About a mile after that, well, you'll see. The view is pretty amazing."

"This is the council place?"

Carlos nods. "The Narragansetts lived here for hundreds of years, you know. They had some spectacular places."

They walk without talking. Traffic passes them continually on the road, which has no sidewalk beyond the town limits. They keep to the right, going single file. The day is cool but bright, the kind of fall day when city people drive out to see the leaves. A smell of wood smoke hangs in the air. From somewhere, out of sight, comes the high whine of a power saw. Someone is clearing land, getting ready to build a new house, maybe. There's been a lot of construction in the area lately. Everywhere you look, land is up for sale, and it's selling. New families are moving in, commuters with city jobs. Providence and its business-park suburbs are just a twenty-five-minute drive up the highway.

"Here's the trail," Carlos says suddenly. "And look who's here."

Parked in a sandy turnout across the road is a red Volkswagen Bug, filled to the roof inside with newspapers, clothes, plastic bags of unidentifiable junk.

"Queenie," Joelle says. "What's she up to?"

"She goes walking, I guess. I've seen her car over there a few times. I've never run into her, though. She must take other paths."

"My aunt says she's a descendant of an early tribe around here."

"I heard that. If it's true, I guess she'd know her way around. Come on."

They turn off the road, and almost immediately, the atmosphere changes. Even before they get to the top of the first rise, Joelle feels the long arms of the forest close around her, shutting out the road noises. She follows Carlos along the trail, which is thick with fallen leaves in places but in others is clear and wide, a well-beaten track.

"Is this an Indian trail?" she asks.

"No. It's part of the North–South Trail that goes up to Massachusetts. Hikers use it. See those blue marks on the trees?"

"Yes," she says. "I've heard about this. I've never done much hiking."

"Before my brother died, my father used to bring us here," Carlos says, turning around to speak to her. "That's how I got to know it. Now I come whenever I can."

"Your brother died?"

Carlos shrugs. "He was a lot older than me." He turns and walks on. "Anyway, it's a great feeling to be out here by yourself," he says over his shoulder.

Joelle nods. She can see he doesn't want to go into what happened to his brother, which is a relief, actually. If he doesn't tell about himself, then he won't expect her to do the same. The trouble with getting to know people is that they start being nosy.

They think they have a right to ask you whatever they want.

"It's so quiet here," she says, to let Carlos know it's okay if they don't talk.

It isn't really quiet, though, once you start listening. Leaves rustle, tree limbs creak, birds cry out, small feet scurry through the underbrush.

"Am I hearing water?" Joelle asks suddenly, cocking her head.

"Cowaset Brook," Carlos answers. "It's named after an Indian sachem."

"A what?"

"Sachem. A chief."

A minute later they come upon a rocky stream rumbling noisily through the woods. The water is bright and clear, joyful-looking as it tumbles along over rocks, against fallen branches. Joelle wishes she could stop for a minute to dip in a hand or a toe, but even as she slows down, Carlos warns her, "There isn't time. We have to keep moving if we want to be back by dark."

"Why? Are wild animals out here?" She's heard an uneasy tone in his voice.

Carlos shifts his gaze off to the left and stares for several seconds into the forest there. "Nothing like that," he says. "It's easy to lose your way in the woods after the sun sets. Also, we wouldn't be safe going back on the main road. Drivers can't see you in the dark."

Joelle nods, thinking what a careful person he is. She's already noticed that he's wearing a first-aid kit on his belt. There's a water bottle, too.

"Were you in the Boy Scouts or something?" she asks, kidding him a little.

"No," he flashes back, "were you?" He turns around and takes a comical gawk at Joelle's Alpine five feet nine inches.

It's the first joke he's ever made off her, and they both laugh. "No offense," Carlos says, looking worried.

"No way," Joelle assures him. "That makes us equal."

They walk on with a good feeling between them. The sun plays hide-and-seek through the trees, ducking out of sight, then blazing up suddenly in their faces as they come over a rise or into a clearing. Soon the trail splits, and they fork off to the left on a narrow path, hard to see.

"Almost there," Carlos says.

The ground rises steadily now, and for ten minutes they push ahead without speaking. Joelle entertains herself by imagining she is an Indian girl walking lightly along the path. Like a shadow, she passes, fitting each step exactly into the footstep of the person in front of her, a way of walking her Indian mother taught her to deceive enemy trackers. (There's no telling where she really picked this up. On TV, maybe?) She doesn't make a sound. Even the animals and birds don't hear her coming. Suddenly, up ahead, the cloddish stamp of intruders' feet crashing through underbrush rings out! White men! In her sacred land! The Indian girl must run and warn her village. Like an antelope, she springs away, back toward the rushing brook. She must not be seen. She must not cry out. She must run and run and . . .

"*What* are you doing?"

Carlos has turned around and is staring at her.

"Oh!" Joelle, caught in the act of springing like an antelope in place, comes to earth with a thud and grins sheepishly. "I had this sudden vision."

"Of *jumping*?"

"Forget it. Are we getting there?"

They are. Around the next bend the forest falls away, and with no warning, Joelle finds herself on the edge of a cliff—a stupendously high cliff with views that shoot off to distant horizons. Below, a wide, multicolored carpet of forest spreads across the valley floor. The lowering sun shines on it, firing up bright yellows, oranges, and reds. Islands of green linger in places.

Beautiful but . . . glancing down, Joelle realizes she's within inches of the sheer rock drop-off. For a moment she's terrified, too paralyzed to breathe. It seems as if the abyss below is beckoning, trying to draw her down. Some insistent hand has taken hold of her and is pulling her forward. With effort, she resists and drags herself away.

"I've never liked edges. I always think I'm going to fall," she tells Carlos apologetically.

He isn't intimidated. He sticks his hands in his jeans pockets and stands proudly at the brink.

"A hawk," he says, pointing to a winged form soaring regally in front of them.

Joelle nods. Away from the edge she feels safe, and the beauty is overwhelming. She never knew this was here. All this time, living down in town, she never knew. It's as if she's walked through a door into another world.

"Where is Marshfield?" she asks.

"You can't see it from here. We're looking west. You can imagine the grand council meetings the Narragansetts probably had up here. And at night, around a fire, they held ceremonies and big celebrations."

"Like what?"

"I don't know. Mask dances and rites of passage. The Sioux had a whole system of beliefs about the world that have been passed down and studied, but nobody knows very much about what the Narragansetts believed. They were killed off too fast."

"I'd like to come here at night sometime," Joelle says wistfully. "Wouldn't it be great to camp here, under the stars?"

Carlos nods. They look out at the horizon again and listen to the sounds a forest makes when it's alone, undisturbed, living free of civilization. Distant caws, windy sighs, a sudden crash from the underbrush. But also, beneath these, Joelle hears a more elemental noise: a low, continuous moan or howl that seems to come from all compass points at once, out of the depths of the valley before her. She thinks: *Is it the pure voice of the land speaking?* She looks at Carlos and smiles.

"This isn't the only place like this," he says. "There are a lot of lookouts in this area."

"I'd like to see them."

"There are boulders that still have Indian markings on them and caves they used during hunting trips. The Narragansetts built their villages in swamps. I could show you where. Swamps protected them from their enemies. Only they knew the paths to get in."

Joelle nods, happily. This is a kind of history she can deal with. "Where is Connecticut?" she asks.

"You're looking at it." Carlos points toward a forested rise. "The state line's not very far away. In fact, Massachusetts is only about fifteen miles north of here. We could probably see that, too, on a really clear day."

"Were there Indians up there, too?"

"Other tribes, not so powerful as the Narragansetts. They traded with them. A lot of the roads we drive on are old Narragansett trails. The Indians knew the best routes, where to cut through valleys and ford rivers. The first white settlers had it easy. They just followed the trails that had been here for hundreds of years. Then they moved in, built towns, and took over."

"Not without a fight," Joelle says. "The Indians fought back, right?"

"Not at first," Carlos says. "They welcomed the settlers. The Narragansetts were generous. They thought the land was for everybody, that it was meant to be shared."

"Well, that was a mistake."

Carlos nods sadly. "They were the first tribe around here to come in contact with whites. They didn't have any idea what they were up against. They didn't know that a whole other civilization, ten times more powerful than they were, was getting ready to move in on them from across the ocean."

"If they'd known, would it have made a difference? Could they have worked something out?"

Carlos considers this question and shakes his head.

"The English didn't want any deals. They were very religious and thought God meant them to take over. The Indians would have lost everything no matter what, just the way they did, not only here, but all across America."

"The way you did, you mean," Joelle points out. "Your people."

Carlos pauses again. "Except I'm not only Indian. I'm part English, too, like the people who killed them. And part Spanish, like the conquistadores who invaded Mexico."

"Spanish! Is that where your name comes from?"

"It's my dad's middle name. My other grandmother was supposedly from Colombia. I'm also part, I don't even know, Polish or something. My mother's family came from Europe. Anyway, I don't feel as if I lost my land. It's much more complicated than that. How about you?"

"Me?" says Joelle. "I'm not Indian."

Carlos looks at her. "You might be. How do you know?"

"If I were Indian, I'd feel it, don't worry."

"I don't exactly feel Spanish, you know."

"Look, I'd just know!" Joelle snaps, sending him a warning flash: She doesn't want to go on with this. No one has the right to tell her what she might or might not be. She's deciding for herself, so lay off.

Carlos gets the message.

"I guess you're not, then," he agrees. "Too bad."

"And exactly why is it too bad?"

"Because then we'd kind of be related."

This is such an unexpectedly nice thing to say that Joelle's mind goes blank and she can think of nothing to answer back. She's never thought of being connected to someone that way, by a whole people rather than by what she doesn't have—brothers, sisters, cousins.

They stare out across the land again. Magnificent. Glorious. Trees flare up like live coals in the sun, burn brightly for a second or two, then darken. Farther on, other trees catch fire. Gauzy clouds overhead are causing this effect as they drift in front of the sun.

The sun! They both realize it at once. It's sunk quite low in the sky. Time to go. Immediately!

They take turns swigging from the water bottle, then start off on the narrow path back through the woods.

"Keep close," Carlos says. "I'm going to move."

They walk fast and are soon back at the

fork that leads into the wide hiking trail. Twenty minutes later they are alongside the rushing brook again. Here, glancing worriedly at the sky, Carlos picks up the pace.

Joelle tramps along behind him, not really looking where she's going. Her head is full of the past. The forest is working its silent charm on her again, more mysteriously now because the light is failing. The trees, which were merely netting before, a loose weave sifting the sun's autumnal gold, have turned dense and brooding. A wind has come up. Shadows dance with shadows. It's possible to imagine a group of tawny-skinned figures moving along a path parallel to theirs, slipping silently between the trees.

Suddenly, Joelle sees them. They are warriors returning from a hunting trip up north, and they've been successful, as in the mural at the library. They are carrying two deer and also a bunch of snared rabbits and a fat wild turkey. The outlines of this bounty are clear, slung over their shoulders and strapped to their backs. Tonight, around a fire, the people of their village will have plenty to eat. Everyone will celebrate, and news from the north will be reported. Perhaps a great chief has died or an important marriage has occurred. Or is it that a company of pale-faced strangers-from-across-the-sea has been sighted marching inland from a northern beach? A high council will be called at the overlook, and chiefs of surrounding tribes will be invited to come for a discussion of the matter.

From the theater of her imagination, Joelle watches longingly as the hunters slip away toward their camp. Their lean shapes melt into the gathering darkness, and suddenly—the feeling lunges up in her—she wants to go with them. She would like to see their camp, sit by their fire, eat their food. For a step or two she even forgets herself and veers off after them, nearly plunging into thick brush bordering the path. Just in time, she stops herself. What was she thinking?

She runs to catch up with Carlos. He is ahead walking steadily when, all at once, he comes to a halt and takes a long look off to the right. Joelle, racing up behind, almost crashes into him.

"What was that?" he asks.

She listens but hears nothing, only the

sound of the wind kicking branches over-head. "What?"

"A scream. Did you hear it?"

Joelle shakes her head. "No. Nothing."

Carlos listens again. "Somewhere over there is a mass of glacial boulders called the Crying Rocks," he says. "I visited them once with my father."

"What were they crying about?" Joelle jokes, then wishes she hadn't. She's getting as bad as Aunt Mary Louise. Carlos is frown-ing. His face, in shadow, has taken on a stern, gaunt look. For the first time Joelle sees, or imagines she sees, a vague outline of his Indian ancestry—something about his nose and the slope of his forehead. He is gaz-ing intently into the forest.

"The story is that when you pass by these rocks at certain times, you hear children cry-ing," he says.

"Children! What children?"

Around them tree shadows flick and twist.

"Ghosts of Indian children," Carlos says. "They were killed there or something. A long time ago. Or maybe it's their mothers who are crying, I don't know."

"It's getting so dark," Joelle murmurs.

In that moment an eerie feeling descends on them both.

"Let's get out of here," Carlos whispers.

They catapult ahead down the wide trail, running and running, not looking back. The forest, speeding past in a blur, turns black and menacing. The wind howls in their ears. Branches claw at their clothes. They keep running. Downhill. Uphill. Through a meadowlike clearing. Downhill again.

After what seems a long time, the ground begins to level out. A faint glow appears ahead of them. They are breathless by now, nearly out of strength, but in another moment the glow becomes a sparkle, then a mighty blaze. They break through the forest's edge. Heart pounding like a drum, Joelle gazes down and gasps with relief. Below is the noisy, smoggy, headlight-clogged road that promises, in this last hour of the waning day, to take them safely home. Who would ever guess it could look so beautiful?

"Well," Carlos pants beside her, "that was exciting!"

They are walking down the incline toward the lanes of speeding cars when Joelle has a thought. She glances across the road to the sandy turnout, but Queenie's red Bug is gone.

"So what is this story about crying rocks?" Joelle asks Carlos lightly as they approach town a half hour later and can walk side by side again. "Who got killed? You kind of scared me back there."

"Sorry." Carlos laughs. "It's nothing, really. An old Indian legend my father told me once, from back when the English were fighting the Narragansetts, I guess. I don't know why I even thought of it."

"You heard something."

"I know. A kind of scream, far off. The wind, most likely."

"I didn't hear anything, just branches scraping together," Joelle says firmly.

"Well, that proves it. It was the wind."

6

THE OVERHEAD LIGHTS ARE TURNED OFF, and the Indian mural is merely a huge, black oblong between the men's and women's bathrooms when Joelle goes to see it, alone, after school, the following afternoon. Something has drawn her here, she's not sure what. Outside the day is dark, rainy, and cold, and not many people are in the library. The library staff, being budget-minded, is keeping lighting to a minimum to save on electricity.

The light switch is on the left. Joelle flicks it. Above her the mural springs to life. The women are hoeing and basket weaving. The children are playing with the dog. The white man is examining tobacco leaves that an old Indian man, perhaps one of the tribal elders, has offered him.

The hunters are there, bursting upon the scene with their two deer and the rabbits and the turkey. (Yes, they are carrying rabbits and a turkey, Joelle is amazed to discover. She must have noticed this detail before and stored up the memory without realizing.)

The hunters are bare-chested, and their heads are shaved except for a stiff bristle running back from their naked crowns, exactly the way she saw them in the forest. Or rather, the way she imagined she saw them. It is all a little strange. She almost feels that she is meeting these men again, for a second time.

Off to the side the two Indian girls with the long, black braids are standing as still as statues, their hands clasped tightly together. Joelle doesn't look at them directly at first. She's afraid of what she might see. But after a minute she can't keep her eyes away and allows herself a quick glance, then an all-out stare.

Immediately, there it is again: the snake-like slide of a memory. But it twists away before Joelle can make sense of it. In its place she feels an odd rush of friendship for

the girls, as if she's known them somewhere, in some other place. They are wearing finely beaded bands low on their
foreheads and long deerskin dresses over
deerskin leggings. Who are they? Why do
they seem so real?

There's nothing in the mural to answer
these questions. The painting has no depth
and probably no meaning, either, beyond its
symbolic arrangement of stereotypes. It's
pointless to look for more. And yet: Joelle
takes a step back and runs her eyes over the
whole mural. There is something here that
attracts her, more than ever now that she's
been in the forest with Carlos.

After a few minutes she goes back to the
front of the library and types the words
"Narragansett Indians" into the catalog com-
puter. Several titles are listed. She jots them
down before entering another phrase under
the same heading: "The Crying Rocks."

It's a long shot, and she's not much surprised when nothing pops up. They're a
local landmark, probably, the scene of a
ghost story passed down through gen-
erations to explain some odd outcropping
of stone.

Still, it's interesting that a place like that, lost in the woods, below the radar of official history, could be powerful enough to survive as a memory all this time. What happened there so long ago? Joelle checks out three books about Narragansett Indians and departs the library.

Sometimes it seems to Joelle that she can remember her trip across the country in the freight car. She doesn't look for this memory. It arrives unannounced: a certain dark aroma filling her head, a feeling of enclosure, and a sense of speed.

If she isn't in school then, or out doing something in town, she goes to her room and sits cross-legged on her bed. She closes her eyes and lets the freight train carry her away. *Clickety-clack*. The train wheels clip over the track.

The heavy sliding door of the freight car hasn't been closed all the way. There is just enough room for Joelle to sit in the opening, swinging her legs over the edge and watching the country go past. The freight car's metal floor has been riding in the sun and feels warm against her bare legs. She looks out for hours at fields speeding by, at farms and towns, into the tangled underbrush of forests, at mountains in the distance rising and falling and fading away, at white clouds above them floating across the sky.

A happy feeling comes into her, pours through her skin with the warm sunlight, until her body becomes as loose and flexible as rubber. It isn't as bad on the freight train as someone might think. She's not lonely and doesn't miss anybody. There is even a feeling of relief, as if she's escaped from something or left a difficulty behind.

She has food in a brown paper bag: peanut butter and jelly sandwiches on soft white bread that somebody made for her. She has water in a screw-top jar. There are people who are traveling with her, but they sleep a lot, or maybe they jump off at one of the stops and never get back on. She hardly notices. Instead, a large, long-haired cat has come aboard and keeps Joelle company at night, curled up by her side. When the car rattles too hard or the whistle blows too loud, the animal trembles and looks up at her with wide, terrified eyes. To keep it from bolting, Joelle gives it a piece of sandwich and strokes its long hair.

"I'll take care of you," Joelle whispers. "Stay with me. We'll be safe."

Together they look out the train's big sliding door to where the stars are making pin-prick patterns in the sky. The dark night is as soft as velvet. The cat is warm against her side. They are on their own, going somewhere, flying across vast floors of land between horizons.

Misti, waiting for her behind the hedge the next morning, studies Joelle intently as she crosses the lawn to the sidewalk. She keeps glancing up at her all the way to school, but she doesn't mention Joelle's hair until just before she has to turn off. Then she says: "You have braids."

Joelle smiles and nods.

"They look nice. You look like an Indian."

"Thanks."

"Can you do my hair like that?"

"Sometime," Joelle says.

"Today? After school?" Misti begs. "I could come to your house."

"No!" Joelle says, more sharply than she intended. "I have a lot of homework," she adds, as an apology.

She wouldn't mind doing Misti's hair but doesn't want to get dragged into anything with the others, especially Penny Perrino, who strikes her as not a very nice girl. Several times Joelle has overheard her make sneering comments to Misti: about the clothes she wears, which are from the cheaper department stores; about Misti's family. "Everybody's got the same kind of eyes. All funny-looking," she heard Penny say to her. It reminds Joelle of the way some people look at her in school and around town.

When they reach the elementary school building, Joelle gives Misti a little push on the arm to send her off. "See you later."

"Okay, see you later," Misti echoes, and trudges off valiantly toward the door.

Her small figure looks so innocent and defenseless that Joelle's heart goes out to her, and she almost calls her back to say she'll do her hair. But at the last second she keeps quiet. *After all, it's better not to get too involved,* she thinks. She might start worrying about Misti, feeling responsible for her, which would be dangerous. Why would it be dangerous? Joelle doesn't know, and something tells her not to look into it more deeply.

No sooner has Misti gone through the door than Carlos bounds up beside Joelle like a big puppy, his coat flapping. Obviously, he's had his eye on her. He was hiding somewhere, waiting for an opportunity to talk to her alone. She's not sure she likes this. It's too possessive.

"So, Tonto, I thought we'd lost you," she says in her mocking tone. "Misti was worried when we didn't see you coming up your street."

Carlos smiles and shakes his head.

"I told her you were ambushed by Apaches. Now she's really upset."

"She is not. You're the only one she cares about. What is it with you, anyway? You're the Pied Piper of little girls?" Carlos teases her back. He's getting better at this, actually.

"Ha-ha," says Joelle. "At least I'm not making a total fool of myself crawling around town on my hands and knees hunting for arrowheads all the time."

"No, you're just braiding your hair to look like an Indian squaw."

Joelle narrows her eyes. "Squaw! Forget it. If I'm anything, I'm an Indian sachem. Queen Awashonks of the Sogonites or Weetamoo of the Pocassets."

"Who?"

"I was reading about the Narragansetts last night. Women could be leaders of their tribe. They were known for being smart, and ruthless to their enemies. They *could* be merciful, though—to those who bowed and scraped before them." She gazes down at him regally from her great height.

Carlos grins and nods. He never gets angry, apparently.

They are approaching the school by this time and have joined the flow of other students on the front walk.

"Listen," he says, under cover of the babble. "Do you want to go on another hike? I could show you a cave with ancient Indian markings."

"I want to see the Crying Rocks," Joelle replies. "Do you know where they are?"

Carlos doesn't answer for a second. When she glances at him, he says, too quickly: "I'm not sure I could find them again. I was pretty young when I was there. "

"Aren't they somewhere close to where we were?"

"Maybe. I'm not really sure." This sounds definitely evasive.

"You don't want to go back?" Joelle asks.

"I'd have to ask my father exactly where they are."

"Then ask him!"

"I'll see."

For some reason, Carlos doesn't want to visit the rocks. Well, everyone is entitled to their privacy; no one knows this better than Joelle.

"Okay, let's see the cave, then. I can't today, though," she says, suddenly remembering. "I have to pick up some medicine after school. You know, for my aunt."

Carlos doesn't know. He doesn't know a thing about Aunt Mary Louise. Not about her being sick or about how, this morning, she lost her balance and couldn't get out of bed after Vernon left. Joelle went upstairs and helped her into the bathroom. In the end, she was all right. She even walked down to the kitchen and fixed breakfast for the first time in a week.

Carlos doesn't know any of this, and Joelle doesn't intend to tell him. He has sharp antennae, though, and seems to have detected some worry in her voice.

"Is your aunt okay?" he asks.

"Oh, sure," Joelle announces breezily. "She's just been a little dizzy lately."

"A little dizzy?" He gazes at her with concerned eyes, an inheritance from his father the great doctor, no doubt.

"It's nothing."

"Are you sure? Dizzy can mean something."

"Of course I'm sure," Joelle says.

"But it sounds kind of—"

"Well, it's not!" Joelle bristles, cutting him off. Carlos has crossed the line, the invisible line even she can't see until it's already been crossed. He's getting too close.

"If there's something my father can do—"

"There isn't!"

"He might be able to tell you—"

"Don't worry about it, okay? Just leave it alone," Joelle explodes, now breathing fire.

"Sorry." Carlos backs off. "I didn't mean to—"

"I know!" Joelle shouts over her shoulder. She plunges away down the hall toward her first-period class, the Indian braids beating like two angry sticks against her jacket.

7

AUNT MARY LOUISE HAS LIVED MOST OF her adult life here in Marshfield, on the western edge of Rhode Island. She grew up in the area, too, just across Narragansett Bay, in Tiverton, where some of her brothers and sisters still live. Joelle remembers when they used to drive over to see them, on holidays usually, a couple of times a year.

They haven't visited recently. Vernon took a dislike to Aunt Mary Louise's family, who are all devoutly religious. He called it the Bible Belt over there because they talked about the Lord Jesus all the time and tried to convert people. At meals everybody had to hold hands and bow their heads before taking a bite. Joelle still remembers getting a hard slap on the arm from one of Aunt Mary

Louise's sisters when she tried to eat a piece of corn bread too soon. Vernon had shot out of his chair and yelled at the woman. He'd snatched Joelle away, over to his side of the table.

"They don't like her looks and they never will. She's not one of them, thank God," Joelle heard him tell Aunt Mary Louise in a low voice on the way home in the car. "You keep her away."

After that they never went back.

"Don't you wonder how they are?" Joelle asked Aunt Mary Louise a few times, after they stopped going.

"Oh, they're doing okay. I get a card now and then."

"I mean, do you ever miss seeing them, in person? They're your family."

The question Joelle was really asking was: If you're related to someone, by blood, do you have feelings for them that you can't help, that are just built in? Is there some genetic thread that keeps you connected? Back when she was Misti's age, Joelle, unrelated by blood to anyone she knew, had begun to wonder.

"I do miss them," Aunt Mary Louise had

admitted, "but not enough to go without you. And if we went, I'd have to lie or Vernon would be mad. Then he'd probably find out, and I'd have to lie about telling the lie, and on and on. Once you start that, you're headed down to hellfire."

Even after being married all these years to Vernon, who thinks all religions are frauds that prey on human weakness—"Oh, they pray, all right. They prey and prey," he says—Aunt Mary Louise has kept up a private belief. She doesn't attend church anymore, but her faith shows in little remarks like this one about hellfire. Heaven and Hell are real places to her. Angels exist. You can believe in God without necessarily doing anything about it, she told Joelle. God looks down and watches over you. He knows who you are from what you keep in your heart.

"Does He know where you came from, too?" Joelle asked, back when she was little. "Does He remember, even if you don't remember yourself?"

"Well, of course," Aunt Mary Louise had said. "That's one of His main jobs. Things get mixed up down here on Earth, as you know. People get lost. Up there it's all straightened out."

"You mean, I'll meet my Chicago mother up in Heaven?"

"You will, I'm sure. And I hope she'll be the better for it."

These days Joelle doesn't believe in Heaven as a real place anymore. The idea of a large, saintly person hanging around in the sky, looking down on her, strikes her as silly. Still, she often has a feeling that she's part of some larger story, that unseen eyes are upon her, watching what she does. They are accepting eyes, not the critical ones she meets in the halls at school, and they do seem to look from another world, a place mysteriously hidden from her view.

"Did you know there are giant cliffs near here where you can look out for miles, even into Connecticut?" she asks Aunt Mary Louise when she gets home from doing the errands that afternoon. Aunt Mary Louise is lying on the couch as usual, but she doesn't look too bad. "I just wondered if you knew, since you've lived around here for so long."

"Cliffs?" Aunt Mary Louise says. "Could be. I never walked back up there much."

"Did you ever hear of some Indian place called the Crying Rocks?"

"No. I heard of something like it, though. Wailing Bog, I think it is. Down in South Kingstown or somewhere."

"Well, what is it?"

"Hmm. If I recall, the story is that when folks pass by there, they hear some poor Indian mother wailing for her children, who she abandoned after her husband ran off. This was a while back, a couple hundred years ago. There are a bunch of stories around like that, but there's nothing to them. A flock of wailing geese is what it probably is."

"Why did the woman abandon her children?"

"Who knows? One story is, the father was a white man."

"So?"

"Well, if he was white, she, being Indian, would have been cast out by her tribe for being with him. Mixing blood brought shame back then. I guess some people still think it does. Anyhow, when the white man left, the woman was caught stranded. Nobody would take her in from one side or the other, and her kids were destined to be outcasts too. So she left them in the bog."

"To *die*? Why didn't she just go somewhere else with them?"

"I guess there wasn't anywhere else to go."

"It sounds completely crazy to me. Who would do that to their children?"

"It's only a story, Joelle. Don't get yourself upset."

"I'm not upset! It just sounds dumb!"

"Well, that's right, it is. And if you went to Wailing Bog, you'd see that it's probably not even true. No Indian mother is wailing for anything over there. What you've got is a lot of honkers floating around the marsh, the same as they've been doing for a thousand years."

Aunt Mary Louise rolls over and turns her back to Joelle, signifying that this is the end of the discussion. Joelle lets her rest for a while. Too much conversation seems to exhaust her these days. Finally, she has to go and whisper to her, though.

"Shouldn't we be doing something about dinner?"

"Oh, Lord!" Aunt Mary Louise groans. "Is it that time already?"

"I'll do it, if you tell me what to do."

"No, no. I'm fine!"

She gets up slowly and lumbers upstairs to wash her face and comb her hair. It's amazing to Joelle that, old as she is, she still cares what she looks like. Every evening Aunt Mary Louise puts on lipstick and little dots of cheek rouge. She stands in front of her bedroom mirror, on tiptoes (Joelle has watched her), and takes a turn to make sure her slip isn't showing. By the time Vernon arrives, she'll be in the kitchen cooking, bright and ready to be seen. Not that he notices. Like a robot, he goes to sit on the couch in front of the TV. Or he disappears outside. It's sad how he takes her for granted, Joelle thinks, and how Aunt Mary Louise pretends not to care but goes on giving him sweet smiles and chatting up a storm. This is on a good day, of course, when they aren't having one of their fights.

Today, when Aunt Mary Louise has finished pulling herself together, she comes down with a determined expression on her face, and they set to work in the kitchen. They are well along on Swedish meatballs when they hear Vernon's pickup pull in. Next, instead of the front door opening, they hear the scraping sound of his tailgate going down. Joelle looks out in time to see him take out a cardboard box and carry it around the house to the backyard.

A minute later he's returned for another box and, after that, a third and fourth. Aunt Mary Louise has shut off the stove by now, and they both watch.

"I know what it is. It's the fer-tile eggs," she says at last. "You know, for the chicks. He must have got the heater working out in that new shed."

"What heater?"

"To keep the eggs warm until they hatch. I guess he's going to do what he said. Be a hatchery for the chicken farms."

More than an hour passes before Vernon comes in, via the back door, in his socks. He's taken off his boots and left them outside, an unusual courtesy toward Aunt Mary Louise's floors.

"Well, I got 'em!" he announces, looking straight at her.

"So we see."

"Real good eggs. Disease free."

"I should hope so," Aunt Mary Louise says.

"I'm starting up," Vernon goes on. He

hasn't talked this much in a month. "Three weeks and I'll have my first batch. It's all set out there."

"Wonderful!" says Aunt Mary Louise. "Shall we celebrate? We could go out to eat if you want. I could put these—"

"Nah, it's nothing. Just a beginning." Vernon waves a dismissive hand. He gets a beer out of the fridge and leans up against the sink.

"If this works, your Aunt Mary Louise won't need a sit-down job or any other kind," he tells Joelle. "She can go on resting up forever if she wants."

"Forever! I'm no freeloader," Aunt Mary Louise protests, but in a pleased voice.

"Freeloader!" exclaims Vernon, keeping his eyes on Joelle. "She was never one of them. She worked her whole life. She could've run that entire chicken plant single-handed if they'd let her. They demoted her back to gutting, you know, for having too many good ideas."

"Oh, hush, they did not." Aunt Mary Louise lifts a pot lid and peers in. "Anyway, that's ancient history."

"It is not, it's current history. They said she

couldn't go into managing without a high school diploma. That's what's ruining her health," Vernon continues to Joelle, as if Aunt Mary Louise weren't even there. "She sits around here all day, dwelling on the past."

"I do not!" Aunt Mary Louise says. "I certainly do not bother myself with the past. I put my mind on happier things."

"Books," Vernon says disparagingly. "Read, read, read."

"And what's wrong with that?" Aunt Mary Louise asks, turning up the gas under the meatballs. She swings around to confront Vernon with challenging eyes. Her cheeks are bright pink from cooking, and she looks almost pretty. Vernon stares at her in surprise for a moment, then backs off into the living room.

"Did I say anything was wrong with it?" he throws over his shoulder.

Aunt Mary Louise gives Joelle a grin and raises her eyebrows.

When dinner is ready, they all sit down as usual. Vernon reverts to his silent self while Joelle and Aunt Mary Louise carry the conversation.

"Did you really get demoted?" Joelle asks. She hadn't heard that before.

"Long ago, long ago," she answers. "I haven't always gotten what I wanted in this world. But I have enough," she adds, her eyes proudly on Joelle.

"I'm doing my best, so don't push it," Joelle warns her, half kidding, but half not.

"Don't have to," Aunt Mary Louise replies. "I don't know where you could've got it from, but you came ready-built with all the push you need."

After supper Vernon can't contain himself and has to go out and look at the eggs again.

"Want to take a look?" he asks Aunt Mary Louise eagerly.

"No, thank you. My legs are acting up."

"Oh, come on. It's no distance out there." He's hurt.

"*No, thank you!*" Aunt Mary Louise declares. "Ask Joelle."

"Want to look?" he asks her.

"Sure," she says, and goes with him. He's like a little kid desperate to show off a new toy.

The shed is at the far side of the yard. Vernon gets a key out of his pocket and unlocks a padlock on the door. Inside it's bright and warm. The clean smell of new lumber fills the room.

"See?" he says, pointing. Laid out on several long tables are rows of white eggs, neatly arranged under strips of low lighting.

"Nice," Joelle says. "Come Easter, we can have a regular egg-dying party out here."

"Oh, no." Vernon shakes his head seriously. "These eggs are fertile. They're worth a mint. See that lock on the door? No foxes in here, not the two-legged or the four-legged kind."

"I'll pass the word," Joelle says, grinning. Vernon nods, pleased as can be. He walks around a table and stops on the other side, gazing down with satisfaction.

"Where did you get them?" she asks, more to keep the conversation going than anything.

"The eggs? A place over yonder. They come from good hens," Vernon says. "Don't worry, they're disease free. I made sure."

"How did you do that?" Actually, she's kind of curious to know.

"I checked real good," Vernon says. "I drove over there and looked at the hens they come from, how they live, what they eat. I'm careful that way. Nobody's going to give me any bad eggs without me knowing."

He looks across at her with a fierceness that, as their eyes meet, suddenly gives way to something softer, almost fatherly. Joelle stares at him. It's so unusual for Vernon to show his feelings.

"I know about you, too," he adds abruptly. "I bet you never guessed that."

"Know what?"

"Mary Louise is right. You come from good stock. Don't listen to anybody that tries to tell you different."

"What stock?" Joelle says.

"Nevermind. That's all I'm saying."

"Why?"

"It just is." He comes around the table and makes for the door. Joelle follows him out, watches him put the padlock in place and lock up. They start walking back toward the house.

"When did you find this out about me?" she asks him.

"Before we brought you home."

"What did you do, drive to Chicago or something?"

"Chicago. Ha!"

"But didn't I come from there?"

Vernon looks over at her. "All I'm saying is, you're okay, you can hold up your head with anyone. I didn't even mean to tell that much. Those eggs got me into it. Don't ask me anymore, and don't go asking Mary Louise. She doesn't know anything."

"But—"

"No more, I said!" Vernon strides ahead across the yard. He disappears into the house, letting the kitchen door slam behind him.

This conversation has a strange effect on Joelle. Afterward, for several days, she finds herself divided in two. Half of her understands clearly what Vernon said and feels an urgent desire to get to the bottom of it. If not Chicago, where is she from?

The other half is vague and lazy and can't be bothered to take action. Even odder, whenever the clear half starts to get up steam to do something, the lazy half shuts it down. It has the final say, apparently, and Joelle can lie for a whole afternoon on her bed reading or sleeping, keeping herself vague. Why does she need to know more, anyway? the vague half asks. Chicago is deep in her bones. It's one of the main facts she's always depended on, a name she's attached herself to, and not only that, she's imagined living there.

She knows what the tall buildings of her apartment house looked like. She's seen Chicago on TV, maybe even those same buildings. They're the kind with layers of little porches going up the outside, a porch for each apartment, one on top of the other. On the inside, elevators take you up twenty, thirty, forty floors to wherever you live. She's made the trip up in her mind more than a few times, as she probably did in real life back when she was three years old or whatever. These imagined trips are so clear that perhaps something in her really *is* remembering.

She may have been young, but she knew how to get around. She could work the elevator buttons. From some corner of her forgetfulness, the button marked "3" always looms up, and she stands on tiptoes and presses it. Then, *whoosh*, the elevator rises, stops, she gets out and turns right, toward the door at the end of the hall.

After this things become foggy. She has never actually gone through the door into the apartment beyond. Just as dreams have places in them where the dreamer is repeatedly stopped, Joelle has never been able to imaginatively cross this threshold. What is inside? She has no idea. No feelings about it either, good or bad. Whatever memories were there have been erased. The territory is a blank—terra incognita, as the early explorers' maps say about land that had yet to be discovered. America, for instance.

Joelle's lazy side is persuasive, but as the week goes by it begins to loosen its grip. Curiosity, biding its time on the borders of her mind, finally wins out. After dinner one night she finds herself accosting Aunt Mary Louise, though she feels a deep sense of uneasiness about it.

"Vernon thinks I didn't come from Chicago," she says while Vernon is out tending his eggs.

"Well, that's ridiculous. Of course you came from Chicago. Maybe not way back, whoever your people were, but you were born there," Aunt Mary Louise declares with some heat.

"How do you know?"

"It's written down."

"Where?"

"I don't know. Somewhere."

"Well, where? I want to see it."

"I don't know, Joelle! Anyway, the Family Services lady told us. Vernon was there. He heard it too."

"Then, why would he say that?"

"Don't ask me. He's acting crazy lately."

"So it's for sure? I came from Chicago?" Joelle feels the lazy side stretch and swell again.

"It's as sure as I'm sitting here on this couch. You rode on a freight train. That's how you got to the depot where the lady kept you in a box. A story like that doesn't come out of nowhere. Who would think up such a thing if it weren't true?"

"I don't know. No one, I guess," Joelle says sleepily, lazily.

"Well, there you are."

8

THE WEATHER TURNS COLD. IN THE mornings Misti waits for Joelle in a hand-me-down snow jacket, limp from a hundred washings, and rubber boots whose toes have cracked and collapsed. She wears grubby wool mittens and no hat. Her breath smokes when she breathes. Joelle tries to get out there fast so she won't freeze to death.

"You don't have to wait for me every day, you know!"

"I know," Misti says through icy lips. She is the least complaining of children. Although they've never spoken about it, Joelle knows her family is often hard up. Her father has problems holding down a job and lately seems to have disappeared completely. Now Mrs. Martin, a tiny Japanese woman who never smiles, works at the dry cleaner's. There are several older kids who do after-school jobs around town. Last spring, when Aunt Mary Louise heard through the grapevine that the Martins were going through a bad spell, she packed up a basket with a twenty-pound turkey from Vernon's ranch all cooked and stuffed. This was how Misti first fixed her attention on Joelle, who helped carry the turkey into their house.

"If it's cold or snowing or something, you should just go ahead. I'm not always ready," Joelle tells Misti now, on the sidewalk.

"I like to wait," she says.

"Where's your hat? It's freezing today."

"I forgot it."

Something has happened to Misti's hair. It's been gathered into two strange clumps that stick out unevenly from either side of her head. Joelle takes a minute to figure it out, then she sees: They're braids.

"Did you do those yourself?"

"Yes. But they didn't come out too well. I wanted them to look like yours."

"They're not that bad."

"Everybody has them! You'll see! Penny's mother did everybody's hair yesterday."

"Except for yours?"

"No, because I wasn't invited," Misti admits.

"Why not?"

"Sometimes Penny doesn't invite me. You have to wait for her to tell you if you can come. She can cut people out if she wants."

"Who else gets cut out?"

"Well, just me, usually."

"Why would she want to cut you out?"

Misti shrugs uncomfortably and, blinking fast, glances off to one side. "She said I don't look right," she answers softly.

Joelle sighs. "I think Penny is a rat."

"No, she's not. She just thinks everyone in the group should look like a princess. If someone doesn't, it's ruined for everybody."

This remark so sickens Joelle that she stops Misti in the middle of the sidewalk, whips off her gloves, and says: "Stand still, so I can do your braids." Then, working as fast as she can in the freezing cold, she unsnarls Misti's clumps and braids them properly all the way down, fastening them neatly with the elastics on the ends.

"You know, I'm not what you think I am,"

Joelle tells her fiercely when she's finished. "If you want to know the truth—"

Misti has taken off her own mittens and is feeling her braids with her bare hands. "Wow, these are great! Thank you so much!" she interrupts. "Now maybe Penny will invite me again. Guess what? Two more people joined our club!"

"What club?"

"The Secret Princess Club. That's what it's called. Elizabeth Glass even quit ballet so she could come. Her mother didn't want her to, but she did anyway. Penny is the president. She thinks she might be adopted too, like you. She can remember some things that happened to her before, in another land."

"Oh, sure."

"She can! She remembers that she lived in this castle with a lot of horses. She thinks she learned to ride, and that's how she knows how to ride now."

"*Does* she know how to ride?"

"Yes!" Misti says. "She knows everything, even though she's never taken riding lessons. She wants to, but her mother won't let her."

"Have you ever seen her ride?"

"*No*, because she hasn't ridden *here*," Misti

says, exasperation entering her voice. "She rode before, when she lived in the castle with her other family, before she was adopted!"

For a moment Joelle is tempted to clue Misti in to the real world. She'll have to find out sometime, not only about nasty manipulators like Penny Perrino, but also about adoption itself. *I was rescued from a crate at the railroad station,* Joelle wants to tell Misti. *I don't even know who my real parents were.*

But when she looks down at Misti's thin jacket and cracked rubber boots, Joelle sees she can't tell her that. Misti doesn't need to hear that story, not yet. There's enough hard fact in her life already. When you're young, you need to believe in something magical, like secret princesses. Something with possibilities. For whatever reason, maybe only because they both look different and seem to come from "somewhere else," Misti has chosen to believe in Joelle. It would be mean to tell her the truth.

They pass the road that Carlos lives on, and both turn their heads at once to look. Sometimes he's far down, just a dark blot coming; sometimes he's close. But he's usually there, walking with his methodical gait along the sidewalk.

Today he's not in sight. Misti looks up to see how Joelle is going to take this, but Joelle is determined to show her nothing—as if there were anything to show! She makes her face stiff and impenetrable until Misti glances away. They plod along silently, side by side, through the cold.

———————

The truth is, out of sight of her legion of worshippers, Joelle and Carlos have met fairly often during the past few weeks. It has nothing to do with romance, at least in Joelle's view. The two of them have been studying Narragansett Indians. They've even gone arrowhead hunting after school, sneaking out the side gym door while the Secret Princesses stupidly waited in front.

Last Saturday, despite the cold snap in the weather, they'd gone hiking in another wilderness area on the other side of Marshfield. Carlos had showed off the cave he'd been talking about, which looked disappointing at first, a shallow dip in a rock wall, nothing like the real cave Joelle had been anticipating.

"Where are the Indian markings?" she'd demanded.

They were nearly invisible, reddish scratchings on the stone that she never would have noticed by herself. But once seen, they jumped out at her with an almost magical clarity. One was of a long-legged deer pausing and listening, its head tilted in a most lifelike way. A second showed a chunkier animal, perhaps a beaver or a woodchuck, hunkered down self-protectively. Behind them the shape of what was clearly a human figure stood upright, both arms raised toward the sky.

"How old are these?"

"My father said they could be anywhere from five hundred to a thousand years old," Carlos answered. "He showed me this place a long time ago, and I've kind of kept track of it. Not many people know it's here."

"What do the animals mean?"

"Nobody knows for sure. It could be something like what the Sioux thought. Their belief was that they were only borrowing the lives of the animals they killed. All creatures were their brothers and sisters, with souls that had to be protected and kept alive. The Sioux had to eat, though, so before a hunt they'd draw pictures like these of the animals they were going to kill. Then, afterward, they'd bring back some of the animal's blood, or part of the body, and put it on or near the drawing. That way, the dead animal's soul could reenter its old form and live again."

"A sort of life-recycling operation," Joelle had joked.

"And a way of saying thank-you."

She'd nodded. "I like that. It's a good way to think. Respectful of living things."

The following Saturday the temperature rises and another hike seems possible. Then, about midmorning, the sky darkens and rain begins.

"You can come to my house," Carlos suggests on the phone. He has actually dared to call her.

But Joelle doesn't want to. Though she doesn't say so, she's afraid that going over there would make things too personal. He's never been to her house, either, and she doesn't plan to invite him.

"Can't we meet somewhere else?" she asks him.

"How about the library?" Carlos suggests. "We can do some more research on the Narragansetts."

"Okay. Hold on a minute while I check for royal spies."

"The Princesses? Don't they ever give up?"

"Saturday is their big day. They run relay races to the front door. *Uno momento.*"

Joelle puts aside the beaded headband she's been weaving on the living-room floor, gets up, and peers through a front window. Out near the street she spots a huddle of wet and miserable-looking girls under a tree, taking instruction from Penny Perrino. Misti is not among them, she notices.

"They're here," she reports back to Carlos. "In the rain. They all have Indian braids lately, have you seen?"

"Way to go, Weetamoo. Now you have a tribe."

"Ha-ha, very funny."

"Can you vamoose out the back door?"

"*No problema.* I'll disguise myself as a *paraguas* and be there in half an hour."

"What's a *paraguas*?"

"An umbrella, *estúpido*. In Spanish. Did you miss it on the test?"

"Oh, that *paraguas*. I certainly never heard it pronounced that way. Mrs. Correja would go into meltdown if she heard you."

"Your accent isn't so hot either!"

"Peace, *amigo*. I'll see you at the library. *Adiós*."

"*Au revoir*, Tonto!"

Back in the stacks, near the long mural of the Narragansett Indians, Carlos and Joelle sit on the floor, whispering and reading. Open books are spread around them. They are continuing their research.

"So they weren't short, they were tall," Carlos says in a low voice. "Look at this passage. Eyewitnesses who first saw the Narragansetts said they were taller than any of the white men."

"Hmm." Joelle takes the book from him and reads to herself the report of the Italian navigator, Giovanni da Verrazano, in 1524:

We saw about twenty boats full of people who came around our ship, uttering many cries of astonishment. . . . This was the finest looking tribe, and the handsomest in their costumes that we have found on our voyage. They exceed us in size. . . . Among them were two kings more beautiful in form and stature than can possibly be described. . . . Their skins are of a tawny color. Their faces are clear-cut, their hair long and black; their expression mild and pleasant. . . . They are very generous, giving away whatever they have. We formed a great friendship with them.

"See?" Carlos says when Joelle looks up.

"See what?"

"Well, you have to admit, it sounds like you. Tall, black hair. And now, with that headband . . ."

Joelle scowls at him.

"Except maybe for the mild and pleasant expression," Carlos tells her, mildly and pleasantly. "I think you're generous about giving away what you have, though."

"What could possibly make you think that?"

"I heard you gave Misti a necklace."

"Just a stupid thing I made out of beer-can tabs in fourth grade. I had to. Penny Perrino told her she didn't look like a princess."

Carlos smiles a knowing smile. "You're a softy," he says. "Read this!"

Joelle reads:

> *Native Americans showed unusual fondness and tenderness for children, a practice criticized by early Puritans who believed their liberal approach to child-rearing undermined discipline. Early New England observers were constantly astonished, however, by the uniform good health and high intelligence of native youngsters, among whom deformities, handicaps, and disease were rarely seen.*

"Beautiful people," Carlos says when she's finished.

"Is that supposed to mean something?"

He shakes his head, smiling.

Joelle puts up a good front, but she never really feels angry at Carlos. He's an interesting person, with a lot of knowledge stored away in his mind and new facts always pouring in. Admittedly, they are facts about weird things—seventeenth-century Indians, arrow-heads, woodland trails, and so forth—but you have to admire his spirit, not to mention his powers of retention. He remembers everything he reads, down to the tiniest details. For instance:

"I keep looking at that mural and wondering what's true and what isn't," Joelle says. "Do you think Native Americans had dogs back then?"

"They had them," Carlos replies. "They were wiry and quick, like small wolves."

Joelle, addressing the mural: "So much for you, Mr. Stereotyping Artist. Your dog up there looks like an overfed Pekingese!"

Carlos, doing his best not to laugh out loud: "The Narragansetts loved and respected their dogs. They trained them to lie in the bows of their canoes and to leap out after geese or ducks they'd shot."

"How do you know all this?"

"I read it in *Indian New England Before the Mayflower*, page fifty-seven."

"Come on! You remember the page number?"

"It might have been fifty-eight."

"You're kidding, right?"

Carlos looks at her with a teasing grin.

He may joke around, but he never insults her. Somehow he's become aware of, and learned to avoid treading on, her sensitivities, including those she hardly admits to herself. Aunt Mary Louise's tiredness, for example. And how Joelle doesn't like to talk about herself. He's careful about intruding on her, too, knows that she doesn't want him hanging around all the time. She needs her space.

Carlos doesn't even seem to care that he's shorter than she is. (He is, but only by about an inch and a half, it's now been established.) If someone doesn't mind that he's shorter than you are, and maybe even likes it, you know he probably won't betray you behind your back.

"Read this," Carlos says now.

Joelle reads:

> On December 18th, 1675, General Josiah Winslow and an armed company of some thousand colonial troops took by surprise a large encampment of Narragansetts in southern Rhode Island.
>
> On a five-acre island in the midst of a great swamp, a primitive wooden palisade

enclosed the Indians' winter quarters, a village of some 500 wigwams. In this place, which was not a fort though later it was called one to justify events, were gathered old men, women, and children, and a few warriors, most having gone to council elsewhere.

With little trouble, the English gained entrance across the frozen swamp, and soon set fire to the mat-and-rush-covered wigwams. A holocaust resulted. More than a thousand Narragansetts perished, many burned on the spot. Others, including children, fled under heavy gun fire into the icy swamp.

Later, Narragansett warriors returning to the scene of the massacre wept piteously for their families, running their hands through the ashes that remained. They sought especially the children who had fled, and called for them on many nights to appear out of hiding, but none were found. How they perished, whether from cold or hunger or some more ruthless hand, was never thereafter known.

Joelle looks up, shaken. "'Some more ruthless hand'! How horrible! Do you know where this happened?"

Carlos nods. "Down in South Kingstown.

The place is still called Great Swamp. There's an old monument that tells the location of the battle, for anybody who's interested. Not a lot of people go there."

"No wonder. It sounds so bad, as if the English went after this village on purpose to wipe out the Indians' families."

"Things were pretty ugly by then, on both sides. The Narragansetts were threatening white settlers too."

"Still, setting fire to a village of women and old men. Shooting the people who ran out, even small children. Then tracking them down, it sounds like . . ." Joelle pauses. "Wait a minute! Could this have anything to do with the Crying Rocks?"

"Shush!" Carlos looks over his shoulder. Joelle's voice is booming out around the quiet library. "It could," he whispers, turning back. "I thought of that too."

"Maybe they tracked the children there and killed them."

"In one of the legends my father heard, some mothers were so afraid their children would be caught and killed by the English that they jumped off the rocks with them and killed them themselves."

"But that's horrible! How could they?"

"It's probably not true. There are a lot of stories about why those rocks cry."

"I want to go see them! You've got to find out where they are!"

Joelle's voice has risen again. She is almost shouting. Carlos puts a hand over her mouth to stop her, and just as he does two girls from school walk around the end of the aisle. He snatches his hand away, but too late. The girls come to a halt and trade knowing glances.

"Well, look who's here, Erin Wolf and Jennifer McTeer . . . in the library, of all things," Joelle says, trying for some damage control. Erin and Jennifer are not known for their great intellectual curiosity.

"We were actually looking for the bath-room," Jennifer admits, giggling.

"Of course, what else?" Joelle stands and points with a flourish. "This way, ladies."

Erin's eyes narrow; she's picked up on Joelle's sarcastic tone. "What are you two doing back here?" she asks.

"Studying," Joelle snaps. "Do you know that word?"

Jennifer giggles again, but Erin's face hardens.

"Studying? Really? Well, don't let us bother you," she says in an insinuating voice as they pass by.

"We won't," Joelle sings out, to have the last word. She glances triumphantly at Carlos. His face has turned a dark red.

"Don't worry about them," she says. "They're total morons. I know because they're in my homeroom."

"Oh, great."

"Why are you so embarrassed? We weren't doing anything. Are you leaving? Come on, Carlos, don't go." He is gathering up his books.

"We'll stare them down when they come back out," Joelle says. "What can they do to us, anyway?"

"Tell everyone."

"Tell them *what*?"

"You can stay if you want. I'm not going to be here when they come out," Carlos announces grimly, and heads off down the aisle. Joelle packs up fast and scrambles after him.

"What is wrong with you?" she cries. But nothing will stop him. He gallops past the children's section, through the Reading

Room, flings open the front door, and is about to race through when a large, ungainly figure looms up in his path. Queenie! She's just making her way inside, out of the rain, a bulging shopping bag in one hand.

"Sorry," Carlos says. He politely holds the door open until she passes, then dashes out. Following behind, Joelle sidesteps Queenie with some swift footwork but catches a heavy whiff of wet wool as she goes by. Or is it wet hair? Joelle stops and looks back at the old woman. It's so familiar, that odor. Where has she smelled it before?

There's no time to think.

"Wait up!" she calls to Carlos. He is already heading away down the street. "Carlos, wait!"

He slows, glances back. At last he stops. But when she catches him, he won't look at her.

"I guess I might have overreacted," he admits.

"I thought you were taking off for Mars."

"I just didn't want to be there when . . ."

"I know. It's okay," Joelle tells him. "I guess I have a thick skin against people like that. They're always looking for ways to make you feel bad."

Carlos nods dismally.

"Listen, I have the perfect solution. We'll take a day off from school tomorrow. By the time we come back, the Dynamic Duo will be on to somebody else. They need live specimens or they lose interest."

"What do you mean, take the day off?"

"We just won't be there. No big deal. It can't rain tomorrow if it's raining today. We could go on a much longer hike. We could even go to . . . you know."

Carlos gazes at her and understands. The Crying Rocks.

"I can't cut school. My parents wouldn't like it."

"You only do things your parents like?"

"No. But they'd be really upset if they found out."

"How will they find out? Listen, I've done it a hundred times. You forge an excuse and bring it to the office the next day. Everybody does it. Your parents used to do it."

Carlos lowers his head and swallows. "I can't."

"Coward," Joelle snaps.

"It's not that."

"Well, what, then?"

He shrugs.

"I know, it's the Crying Rocks. You don't want to go there. What's the matter, are you afraid of ghosts?"

"No."

"Yes, you are. You can't even ask your father where the rocks are."

"Well, so what? I can do what I want!" Carlos explodes. Joelle steps back in surprise. It's the first time she's ever seen him angry.

"You know, you're always pushing people," he goes on. "You think you're smart, but you aren't. Maybe there's something you don't know, something that's none of your business. So forget it, okay? Just forget this whole thing." He turns and marches off down the street.

"Okay, I will!" Joelle bellows after him. She marches twice as fast in the opposite direction. *What a nutcase*, she's thinking. *What a wimp. This is always what happens when I start to be friends with someone. Why do I even bother?*

9

LATE THAT NIGHT JOELLE WAKES UP IN the dark to the sound of rain splashing against her window. Nearby a conversation is taking place.

"Get yourself to a doctor, why don't you?" she hears Vernon say through the bedroom wall.

Aunt Mary Louise replies that she doesn't want to. They get into an argument about it. Not a loud argument. They keep their voices down so they won't disturb Joelle.

Vernon talks in spurts, in a soft, high, out-raged voice. Aunt Mary Louise answers in a lower, more sensible-sounding tone, but in the end, she still won't be persuaded to see a doctor. She's getting better, she says. It would be a waste of money.

"You've got every penny in the chicks. You don't need any big bills right now."

"That's no issue," Vernon tells her. "I have backers who are helping."

"What's this? You never told me. Who are they?"

"Nevermind."

"Oh, I see. Another one of your big secrets," Aunt Mary Louise accuses him.

"Secrets? What secrets?" Vernon asks. Even through the wall, his voice sounds nervous and dishonest.

"You think I'm stupid, don't you?" Aunt Mary Louise says. "You think I'm not onto this story you've cooked up about Joelle. Well, I know more than you think."

"What story?" Vernon asks.

"You know what. It's a wonder I'm not sicker than I am. All your baloney floating around, clogging the air."

At this Vernon gets up with a big crash, goes down to the kitchen, and opens a can of beer. He stands around in there for a while in the dark. The house is small enough that Joelle can always tell what anyone is doing, even if they are standing in the kitchen in the dark.

Finally, Vernon comes back upstairs to the bedroom and starts to put on his clothes, but Aunt Mary Louise begins to cry, so he takes them off again and gets into bed with her. Maybe he puts his arm around her, or maybe they're both just lying there side by side looking up at the ceiling. Joelle can't tell because, after the first creak of bedsprings when Vernon gets in, there's no more noise.

Out in the street a single car goes by, its tires slapping the cold, wet pavement. Joelle feels alone and, suddenly, very scared.

―――――――――

A week passes, during which Carlos does not appear on the morning walk to school, and Joelle studiously avoids making eye contact with him in the halls. In Spanish class they occupy separate planets—Carlos in the back row, bent over his notebook; Joelle up front, staring grimly at Mrs. Correja and the blackboard. After school she heads for the library to put off going home. She hides in the stacks near the big mural, where, if she finishes her homework, she can look for more material on the Narragansetts. She likes best reading the original journals and diaries of the first settlers. Their language is old-fashioned and their accounts often colored by religious and cultural biases, but their impressions of the Indians sound fresh and direct.

Joelle catches sight of native lives ruled by the often brutal realities of existence in the wild, and at the same time of a people full of warmth and humanity.

> *Their affections, especially to their children, are very strong so that I have known a father to take so grievously the loss of his child that he hath cut and stabbed himself with grief and rage.*
>
> —ROGER WILLIAMS, 1643

> *Yet . . . many times they take their children and bury them in the snow all but their faces for a time, to make them the better to endure cold.*
>
> —CAPTAIN CHRISTOPHER LEVETT, 1624

> *When there is a youth who begins to approach manhood, he is taken by his*

*father, uncle, or nearest friend, and is con-
ducted blindfolded into a wilderness, in
order that he may not know the way, and is
left alone there with a bow and arrows, and
a hatchet and a knife. . . . He must survive
there a whole winter with what the scanty
earth furnishes.*

—ISAAK DERASIERES, 1628

*By occasion of their frequent lying in the
fields and woods, they much observe the
stars, and their smallest children can give
names to many of them and observe their
motions.*

—ROGER WILLIAMS, 1643

Over her own head, the mural keeps Joelle
company. Its inhabitants are no longer the
stereotypes she first saw. They've become
familiar: young mothers with plump, brown-
faced babies on their backs; a small boy showing off with a bow and arrow before his
friends; the arriving hunters; the crafty-faced
white men; an old squaw sewing a pair of
new deerskin moccasins. Joelle can't help
inventing plots for them as she stares up. And
there are the two sisters in the shadows for

whom, mysteriously, she feels a kinship. Like her, they look on, unseen and uninvited, at the village activities, though they are part of this native world, and Joelle is not—and never will be, she thinks, with a sadness and longing she doesn't really understand.

———

Early one weekday morning, before school, the telephone rings. When Joelle picks up, she hears Carlos's voice on the other end, abrupt and forced.

"I asked him," he says.

"Who?" It's been so long since they talked.

Carlos pauses, registering irritation. "My father! He told me where the rocks are. We could go today if you want. I think it's supposed to rain, though. Maybe even snow."

"I want to go," Joelle says. "No matter what."

"All right, we'll go. We can leave the same time we usually do for school. Meet me in the park, down at the end behind the trees. That way, no one will see us."

"Carlos, nobody is going to see us. They don't even care!"

"Maybe they don't in your family, but they do in mine."

Joelle imagines him looking guiltily over his shoulder at one or another of his parents. She thinks what a baby he is, always worried that he'll displease or disappoint them in some way. If it weren't for her desperate desire to see the Crying Rocks, she wouldn't even bother with him.

"I can't believe you finally asked your father," she scoffs.

He ignores this insult. "Bring your own water this time. I'm not carrying for both of us."

"Well, if it's going to rain, we'll certainly have plenty of water."

"Just bring it!" Carlos says, and hangs up on her.

An hour later, when they meet in the park, he's still in a huff and barely glances at her from under his baseball cap. She's over her annoyance by then and, excited about the hike, attempts a friendly greeting. When he only frowns back, she lets him march ahead. She knows how it is to feel angry at a person even after they've offered to make peace. She can carry a grudge all day once her back is up, and has a temper worthy of Vernon's, as Aunt Mary Louise has often said. After all, Carlos is a gentler soul.

"I'm sorry," he says, turning back to her as they approach the main road. "I guess I kind of lost it on the phone. I shouldn't have hung up like that."

"No problem. I was acting dumb too."

"No, really. There's something I think I should tell you. You know this place we're going to? It's where my brother fell."

Joelle stops walking. "Your brother who died?"

Carlos nods.

"Is that how . . . ?"

"Yes," Carlos says. He stares at something invisible on the ground. "We were there with my father, and he fell down between some boulders. That's why I wasn't too happy about asking where the place is. I was afraid it might upset my father to think about it again."

"Did it?"

"I couldn't tell. He keeps everything hidden. We've never really talked about what happened. I was only seven."

"It happened at the Crying Rocks?"

Carlos nods. "My father wanted to see them, because of the stories. He was into Native American history. No one had told him when he was young that there was Native American blood in our family, and he wanted Daniel and me to know about it and appreciate it. We'd go on these hikes around here to see places where the Indians had been, like to the cave I showed you and the overlook. We were going to take a trip out West to visit Sioux territory, too, but . . ."

Carlos shrugs. "Afterward my father wasn't interested in going. We didn't go hiking anymore either." He looks up and meets her eyes.

"I'm sorry," Joelle says.

"It's okay. It was a long time ago. I really can't remember it that well. It's like an old dream."

"I mean, I'm sorry I made you ask him. I think you're right, I am too pushy."

"I'm glad I finally did ask," Carlos says. "I've thought about going back. I just never did anything about it."

"Are you sure you want to? Won't it bring up bad memories?"

"I don't think so. Come on, let's get moving. It's cold standing here."

"At least it's not raining," Joelle says, looking up. The sky is overcast but—at the moment, anyway—unthreatening. "Guess what? I brought my own water."

She hefts the knapsack on her back and smiles. The air between them has cleared, and she feels good about Carlos again. She misread him. He's a nice guy.

"I brought a couple of sandwiches, too, ham and cheese. I knew you probably couldn't make anything with your parents watching. My aunt doesn't come downstairs in the morning."

Carlos nods and grins, almost back to his old self. They head off down the road single file, cars buzzing past.

The forest, when they enter it, wears an entirely different face than on their last visit. Where it had been welcoming and glowing with color before, now, without the sun, a feeling of gray emptiness has taken over the atmosphere. The deciduous trees are completely leafless, as stark and bony as old skeletons. Carlos and Joelle wind between them on the trail, their footfalls echoing loudly. All noises are magnified in the vacant spaces that the leaves used to fill, and long before the two reach the brook, they hear its chilly waters racketing over the rocks. When they do arrive on its bank, the water looks dark and oily, churning with wood and forest debris, not anything like the magical place Joelle remembers from a few weeks earlier. She pulls the collar of her jacket up around her neck and follows Carlos when he turns off the trail. Keeping the brook on their right, they head away, through thick brush and trees.

"We're supposed to follow the stream for about two miles," he explains over his shoulder, "then look for a grove of pines. The rocks are beyond that. I think they're pretty big. They're at the edge of a swamp, my father said."

Joelle feels a jab of adrenaline shoot through her system. She's excited, and also a little apprehensive.

"Don't you remember anything about them?" she asks.

"Hardly anything."

"So you didn't hear the rocks crying when you were there before?"

"No," Carlos answers briefly, from which she knows not to talk about it anymore.

A good half hour of tramping goes by before Joelle ventures into conversation again. "We're getting really far out in the woods. I'd be lost without this brook," she says.

"Me too," Carlos admits. "Usually, I can navigate by the sun." He looks up at the heavy gray sky and shakes his head. "Come on, let's speed up."

They attempt a slightly faster clip, but it's not easy. The forest is dense with under-growth, and they are constantly having to step over fallen trees or beat their way through thickets of brambles and bushes to follow the water. The ground is often damp as well, and though the air is cold, mud oozes up the sides of their boots. Carlos is just bending over to take a closer look at where the brook has gone under a heavy growth of bushes when a loud crash erupts from somewhere in front of them and then, frighteningly, a series of smaller crunches and crashes, as of feet departing rapidly.

Joelle turns around, ready to run herself, but Carlos grabs her arm.

"Look over there," he whispers.

Ten yards away a large, antlered buck is standing motionless, a perfect blend of all that lies around him. His colors are the muted browns and grays of the winter forest. His antlers, branching out grandly above his narrow head, might be mistaken for tree limbs. Except for his dark eyes, which stare at them with wary keenness, it's almost as if a patch of woods had risen up and come to life.

Joelle breathes in quietly. Near the buck she begins to pick out the stationary forms of other deer. Like hidden shapes in a jigsaw puzzle, they emerge, their shiny, coal black eyes trained upon her. She and Carlos have stumbled on a good-size herd of does and yearlings in the company of their patriarch.

A full minute passes before anyone moves. Then the buck tosses his head ever so slightly, and as if responding to a signal, the herd bounds off with a flicker of white tails. They vanish like magic into the gray woods. The buck follows, ambling regally.

Carlos laughs out loud. "What a show-off!"

"What a herd!" Joelle is laughing too. "I

didn't know there were that many deer around here."

"Oh, they're taking over," Carlos says, "getting into the suburbs and eating flower gardens. People are beginning to hunt them out there. Here they're safe and they know it. This is an ancient swamp thicket. Not only deer have found hiding places, I'll bet."

"Do you think Indians hid here too?"

"It's exactly the kind of place they'd come—and disappear into just as fast as those deer. Impenetrable to the white man."

"But here we are!" Joelle exclaims. "On their track."

"But we are not white," Carlos tells her solemnly. "I'm a Sioux today."

"All one-sixteenth of you."

"It's enough," Carlos answers. "It's enough to feel things."

She knows what he means. Once again they've come away from the Pilgrim world of whiteness, away from towns and streets, shopping centers and construction sites, chain saws, car horns. She hears the wind kicking up, calling with its forest voice through the trees. She smells the odor of mud under her feet, thick and cold, and the bare-limbed trees' spicy wood. As they turn and plod on through this strange, swampy place, her Indian imagination rises too, and she feels a sort of wildness creep into her.

The pale-faced killers have been left behind. They will never penetrate this world. Like a deer, she has vanished. Her long, straight body is part tree now. Her skin is the color of bark. Her eyes, if she could see them, would have the coal black gleam of a buck surveying his domain. And there, what is that?

She is aware of something else: a shadow-shape following behind her. As they walk the shape is careful to place its feet exactly inside the footprints Joelle is leaving behind, just as their Indian mother taught them, to deceive enemy trackers.

Who is this invisible follower?

It's Joelle's sister, the second Indian girl from the mural. In the story lighting up the stage in Joelle's mind, they are on the run. The murderous white warriors have driven them from their village, and now they must find safety in some other place.

The attack was terrifying. First came a loud pounding of many guns, then the appearance of white warriors running with fire held high on torches above their heads. Suddenly, the whole village was in flames, and screams and wails echoed from all sides.

"Run with me!" Joelle had cried, grabbing her sister's hand. They'd gone to a place where hungry dogs had dug out a tunnel under the rough stockade of tree trunks surrounding the village. Along with other children, they had crawled through the hole and run into the swamp, which was frozen and easy to pass over. Now they were on their way to the big rocks to hide, traveling silently and swiftly through swamp-woods and leaving no extra footprints. The white warriors coming after were poor trackers. Perhaps they would be fooled by the line of single prints and give up the chase. In any case, they will be forced to move slowly, eyes on the ground, which will give the sisters time to reach the rocks.

With blood drumming in her ears, Joelle imagines this drama as she and Carlos plow their way through the dense growth of trees and bushes toward the Crying Rocks. She becomes so wrapped up in her story that a sudden loud shriek over her head makes her jump and shriek herself.

Carlos whirls around. "What's the matter?"

"What was that?"

"Just a bird! Are you all right?"

Joelle nods, embarrassed.

They start off again. Behind her the shadow-shape starts up too, so clearly in Joelle's mind that at times she believes she could turn around and touch her. She imagines her Indian sister's fear and how it's necessary to reach back and take her hand whenever a forest noise startles her. She imagines her sister's face turned to hers with wide eyes that say: "Wait! Don't leave me behind."

"Don't worry, I'll take care of you," Joelle whispers under her breath. "Follow me. We'll be safe."

The terrain has been rising. The ground is becoming harder and drier. Up ahead a darkness looms, and Carlos says: "There's the pine grove. The rocks are a little beyond."

But, having said that, he stands still. The woods around them, which has seemed noisy with their passage, quiets. They hear their own breaths, and see them too; the temperature is dropping. They hear the long, low silence of the forest spreading away from them, for miles perhaps. The stream has disappeared underground into a rise of land. Or rather, as Carlos is now at pains to explain, the spring that is the stream's main source is beneath this rise. He takes a drink from his water bottle and stares around himself again, clearly stalling.

"Let's get going," Joelle says. "I can't wait to see the rocks."

Carlos nods, but he still won't move. He gazes off into the forest. "I remember this," he says. "I know where the spring is. We came this way before."

"Well, where is it?" Joelle asks, hoping to nudge him forward.

"Up ahead, to the right." He stows his bottle, and they walk to a place where the ground is mushy, then farther along to where clear water is bubbling between two rocks. "Fresh water," Carlos says. "Better than the stuff in this store-bought bottle, probably."

Joelle reaches out a cupped hand, traps a bit, and tastes it. "Not bad," she allows.

She has never thought of fresh water actually pouring out of the earth. If she's considered water at all, it's as a thing that lies around in reservoirs and lakes, or comes down in rain to form rivers that eventually make it into the kitchen faucet.

"Okay, I'm ready now," Carlos says. "I'm just remembering so much more about this place than I thought I did."

He leads the way toward the pines, whose trunks are tall, thin, and largely without branches below. Overhead, however, their green-needle boughs have grown into a thick mesh that blocks out what there is of the day's light. They pass into this dim cavern of trees and, walking vaguely downhill for perhaps a quarter of a mile, come out the other side surrounded by outcroppings of giant rocks. And now, Joelle sees, they are at the edge of a real swamp, a vast area of woodland marsh that stretches off to their right. Along this edge a wall of massive glacial boulders rises into view, high over their heads. Carlos has stopped again. His eyes travel up the steep sides of the boulders to take in the hulking gray mass of the monolith above.

"I remember this," Joelle hears him say faintly.

"Is there a way up?"

"On this side," Carlos answers in the same distant voice. He walks across a rocky section of ground. "We went up here."

They climb up, up, between boulders and around them, coming out at the top, where there is now an even broader view of the swamp.

"Which ones are the Crying Rocks?" Joelle asks.

"All of them!" His hand sweeps out to indicate the whole outcropping. "We're here! My father was so excited. I remember he started digging everywhere."

"For what?"

"Bones. He wanted to find evidence of what had started the crying legend, I guess. Daniel was helping him, but they didn't find any up here. That's why my father went down to the swamp. He thought he might find some below the rocks."

"From the mothers who supposedly jumped with their children?" Joelle glances around. She rejects that story. It's not believable.

"I guess so. Daniel kept looking up here,"

Carlos says. "I was pretending to look too, but I wasn't really. I was listening for the ghost children's crying. My father had told me it was probably just the wind blowing through crevices in the big stones. That day I was walking around and listening in different places to see if he was right."

"But you didn't hear any crying. You said you didn't."

"No, I didn't." Carlos pauses. Joelle has taken off her knapsack and is beginning to rummage in it for her water bottle. "Not that kind," he adds.

"You heard another noise?"

He turns his head toward a group of boulders lying off to one side, back from the main ledge.

"I remember something. I was over there," he says, so softly that Joelle barely hears. He walks over to the boulders and hunches down among them, and there is something about the way he crouches, with his knees bent double and his head and shoulders low, that reminds Joelle of the way a little boy might hunch who is wrapped up in his private world, apart from and oblivious to the business of grown-ups. As she watches,

Carlos reaches up and puts his hands over his ears. He flattens his hands hard against the sides of his head.

Joelle drops the water bottle on the ground and walks over. She crouches down beside him.

"Is this where you heard a noise?" she asks.

"Yes."

"Well, what was it?"

Carlos shakes his head.

"Was it . . . ?"

"No wind could make that kind of sound."

"Well, what . . . ?"

"I thought it was the Crying Rocks." He looks up at her. "I was sure it was. It came from there and sounded like them. But . . ."

"It wasn't?" Joelle feels a coldness spread over her.

"I think it was Daniel," Carlos says with his hands over his ears.

"Daniel?"

"He'd fallen and was crying for us. But my father couldn't hear him because he was down below, and I thought it was the crying ghosts and ran away and hid."

Carlos sits down on the ground and gazes

up in horrified amazement at Joelle. "I remember now," he says. "I ran into the forest and covered my ears and hid."

It was later, perhaps thirty minutes later, that he heard his father calling his name and crept out to find him. The rocks had cried terrible cries, he said. They had moaned and wailed. The stories were true. It was not the wind. He was frightened and wanted to go home.

His father smiled. He said he'd fight off any ghosts that tried to come near them. In any case, he'd finished digging and was ready to head home. They could leave anytime. Where was Daniel?

They called and there was no answer. He'd gone off somewhere, it seemed. Perhaps he was visiting an outcropping he'd spoken about before, located farther along the edge of the marsh. They waited patiently for a space of time. When he didn't return, a disturbing thought entered his father's mind. He walked to the rocks' edge and peered over. He came back and asked Carlos a question.

"Where were you when you heard the Crying Rocks?"

Carlos pointed to the boulders.

"And where did the crying come from?"

Carlos pointed.

His father then walked to that place, on the top of another massive bulge of rocks, and called out loudly over the edge: "Daniel? Are you all right? Daniel!"

A faint sound came from below. In an instant Carlos's father disappeared between the boulders, and Carlos could hear him talking to Daniel. He told him to hold on, he was coming. Carlos crept forward and peered over. He saw that his brother was lying wedged into a sharp rock crevice about a third of the way down. His father had found a route and was in the process of climbing there.

Then he was lifting Daniel's head, talking to him, though Daniel was too weak to answer. The fall had opened a broad gash that ran down the left side of his head. He was still bleeding. Blood had pooled in some of the rock fissures around him.

Carlos watched his father take off his own

shirt, tear it in pieces, and devise a bandage to wrap around Daniel's head. He watched his practiced doctor's hands feel Daniel's neck and his back, his legs and his arms for broken parts. He then saw his father perform the seemingly impossible task of lifting Daniel's large body and carrying it up the nearly vertical side of the rocks.

When he reached the top, they set off immediately through the woods, in silence. His father was carrying Daniel in his arms like an enormous, long-legged baby. It took an interminable amount of time to reach the road. They stopped often to rest because Daniel was so heavy. The sodden bandage came undone and had to be rewrapped around his head. Daniel was unconscious by then. His eyes were closed and his skin was ashen.

When they got to the road, no car would stop at first, until they walked out and stood together in the middle and Carlos's father cried, "Help us! Help us!" Someone stopped at last and took them to the hospital, where Daniel was rushed away down a long corridor on a wheeled bed and their father made a series of frantic phone calls. He then disappeared into the hospital himself, leaving Carlos alone in a crowded waiting room.

Carlos's mother came at last to wait with him. After a long time his father emerged from an elevator, still in his hiking shorts and boots. The three of them drove home. Daniel, who had been so large and alive four hours before; Daniel, who had never fallen in his life and prided himself on his sure-footing; Daniel, who was to report to football camp in two weeks to prepare for his first year on the high school varsity team, remained behind in the hospital and died that evening. Carlos never saw him again.

These are the facts that Joelle gradually begins to glean from Carlos's disjointed recounting of the accident. Sitting there by the boulders, he remembers in patches, not in sequence. The scene at the road stopping cars comes before the picture of Daniel's blood pooling into the rocks. The sight of Daniel carried like a child through the woods presents itself to Carlos after he recalls their arrival at the hospital. It seems that Carlos's brain, to protect him from the single crushing burden of the tragedy, has contrived a way to divide the weight into pieces, then has further disconnected and obscured them by hiding them under other memories from intervening years. It's only now, returned to the actual site of the accident, that he can begin to excavate. For the first time he believes he understands the part he played in the drama, the unthinkable part his parents must have known all these years and have studiously avoided speaking about.

"I could have saved him," he says to Joelle. "All this time I never knew. Or maybe I did know and never wanted to believe it."

"You didn't know," Joelle says. "Just leave it at that."

"Why did I hide?" he begs her to tell him. "If I was scared, why didn't I look for Daniel instead? I could have run to my father. He would have come in time, and Daniel might be alive."

"You were a little boy," Joelle reminds him. "The ghosts were real to you. It isn't your fault."

"My father cried that night after the hospital called. He must hate me. That's why he never took me hiking again."

"He doesn't hate you. He understands why you ran."

"How can he? I don't understand it myself. How could I have done this? Why didn't I remember all these years?"

Joelle shakes her head. She can no longer answer. In her throat and behind her eyes she feels a strange pressure, an unwanted tide that threatens to rise and burst into the outside air. She clenches her teeth to force it back.

For a long time they sit where they are, together, saying nothing, listening to an endless concert of tree sounds and bush sounds, bird sounds and wind sounds, swamp sounds and, after a while, the comforting patter of rain falling quietly on the glacial foreheads of the rocks around them. The showers, it seems, have finally arrived.

10

NOT UNTIL THE RAIN BEGINS TO SLANT hard into their faces does Joelle notice it. She pulls the hood of her jacket over her head and looks around belatedly for shelter. Overhead the sky has blackened. Gusty swirls of wind rush past them, carrying a new cold.

Beside her Carlos stirs. "Come on, I know where we can go." He stands up and runs to get his knapsack.

They walk fast toward the edge of the rocks and retrace their steps to a place near their base where it's possible to climb a little and crawl in under an overhanging ledge. Here they are protected and can sit in relative comfort while the rain, now edged with ice, slams down on all sides.

"I noticed this spot on the way up. I thought we might need it," Carlos says in an empty-sounding voice. He still looks shocked.

"Carlos the Careful Camper," Joelle jokes, but he's beyond humor and stares at her bleakly.

Sitting on the earth floor, her back against a wall of stone, she surveys the surrounding landscape. Their view is of the swamp, a soupy tangle of dead brush and reeds, black mud and yellowed grasses. Whenever an especially heavy curtain of precipitation travels across it, a thunderous rattle of husk and stalk drowns out all other noise, even their voices. What did the early Indians do in this kind of weather? Joelle wonders. Caught out in such a storm, did they come here, to this very rock niche, to wait it out as she and Carlos are waiting? Faintly, she hears a low growl of sound ricochet through the downpour.

"Sounds like thunder," Joelle shouts. "Did you hear that?"

Carlos shakes his head.

The wind is tuning up, fortunately blowing the sleet away from, rather than into, their hollow. It's cold, though, and Joelle keeps her hands in her pockets. She's hungry but doesn't mention the sandwiches, which are in the knapsack beside her. Somehow this is not the time for food. Carlos has pulled up his hood and sits huddled against the rock.

While they wait for the storm to subside, Joelle thinks back to her earlier fantasy in the woods, the flight of the children from the English. Now that she's here, in the very middle of the Crying Rocks, she sees that their massive formations would never have provided good hiding. There are no caves or caverns of any depth. The vegetation is sparse above and an impassable swamp cuts off escape from below. If this was really a place of retreat, the people who came here would soon have been trapped. And then what? Joelle presses her body closer to the rock. A low windy moan echoes in the distance.

"There it is again, that noise," she says.

Carlos isn't listening. He's dealing with the weather in his head.

Hoo . . .

"And again. Now it sounds like an animal."

She crawls out from under the overhang on her hands and knees and stares up. A muffled cry reaches her ears, perhaps from the rocks above, though it could be issuing from the swamp.

Or has she invented it? Straining to hear, she crawls even farther forward from the niche, and as she does, her hand comes in contact with a hard object rising up through the swampy earth. It's shaped like a large shell with a crusty surface that, though black with muck, shows streaks of gray white underneath. As she turns it around in her freezing fingers she realizes that it's not a stone or some oddly bleached piece of wood. The substance is bone.

"Carlos, what is this?"

The rain is changing over to ice now and Carlos can't hear her through its crashing descent, though he's only a few feet away. Joelle scrambles back under the ledge. She reaches out to touch his arm and holds her discovery up before him with a shaky feeling that she already knows what it is.

"Carlos, look."

His distant eyes focus and widen, and he

jerks away. The sleet has washed off more mud, enough to see a skeletal scoop of a head and a pair of empty eye sockets. The jaw is missing.

"Where was it?"

"Out there." Joelle points.

"It's human."

"I think so too."

He gazes with loathing at the muddy swamp in front of them and again at the dripping thing in her hand. The wind gusts past, and from above, there is the sound of rocks falling. A small boulder crashes down nearby, making them both jump.

"We aren't safe here," Carlos says.

"But where can we go?"

"Somewhere else. I don't like it here."

"What about—"

Carlos reaches out and grabs the skull from her. Immediately, he is up on his knees, his arm drawn back, and before Joelle can stop him, he hurls it full-force back into the swamp.

"That was evidence! Why did you throw it away?" Joelle shouts at him.

"I don't want any more evidence!" Carlos yells as a great rumble comes from the outcropping above them and more boulders shoot past. "This place is crazy," he screams into the wind.

And so it seems, for now another noise is making its way into the mad cacophony around them. From somewhere above, a single piercing shriek is mounting above the wind's roar. Louder, it comes. Louder and louder. This cannot be confused with imagination. Joelle cowers against the rock. Carlos crouches beside her, looking up. As they listen the shriek broadens into a half-strangled scream that whinnies out across the swamp. Abruptly, it ceases. But a few seconds later another cry begins, its pitch climbing again into that ghastly, throttled wail.

Without waiting another second, Carlos grabs his knapsack and begins to run. Joelle leaps up and races after him. They sprint away from the dark face of the rocks and head for the shelter of the pine forest they passed through before. But even here, under the safe awning of the trees' high branches, they continue to run without looking back. Behind them another frightening scream is mounting, higher, louder, flying after them through the forest like some angry, bodiless monster seeking its prey.

———————

What could make such a noise?

Joelle asks Carlos this question on the telephone that night. They are safe in their own houses, their day away from school having apparently gone unnoticed. The hike home was cold and tiring but uneventful. Outside the driving sleet of the afternoon has abated and been replaced by a light snow that, as they speak, falls with calm determination on the roads and houses of Marshfield. Not enough to interfere with school tomorrow, unfortunately, but a bona fide announcement of a new season. The ground is white. The arms of trees are gently chalked. Winter has come at last.

Carlos is not very talkative. He was truly scared, but won't acknowledge it. Joelle knows he's thinking not only about the screams at the rocks, but about Daniel's desperate cries. They are a single horror in his mind now. His parents are home, bustling around in the background. She hears the scrape of a chair, pots banging, conversation—the sounds of a family preparing for dinner.

"You should tell them that you remember what happened," she urges him.

"How can I?" he asks. "I know what they must think."

"Tell them. You'll feel better. It really wasn't your fault."

"Yes, it was. It was! I'm sure it was!"

What can she say? There's no way to get through to him. He's alone, unreachable. Like the Indian boy left all winter in the forest, he'll have to work things out for himself.

"I keep imagining the Narragansetts who were driven from their village at Great Swamp," she tells him. "If they went to the Crying Rocks, they would have been trapped."

Carlos doesn't answer.

"What I mean is, maybe some mothers *could* have decided to jump with their children, horrible as it seems. They would have felt desperate."

Carlos makes a sound that might mean agreement, or might not.

"Did you feel as if someone was following us through the woods?" Joelle goes on. "I felt someone, on the way to the rocks and on the way home. I think that mural in the library is beginning to get to me. It's on my mind all the time."

Silence.

"So what could possibly have made those terrible screams?"

Finally, Carlos speaks. "Listen, I've still got homework to do," he says. "I also have to forge my excuse for school. I've also got to put my jacket in the dryer. It's soaked. And don't forget about the Spanish test tomorrow on the major cities of Spain."

"Actually, I did forget."

"Bilbao, Pamplona, Madrid, Málaga, Córdoba, Sevilla, Granada, et cetera."

"Etcetera, what city is that?"

"You better study."

"I think your father was right; it was the wind," Joelle says. "There's some way the rocks are formed. The wind passes through and makes a noise—like when we put a blade of grass between our thumbs and blow. It's interesting about that skull I found, though. Did you notice how small it was? And there was a crack that ran down the middle of the forehead. I think—"

"I can't talk anymore," Carlos interrupts, and hangs up fast.

———————

The next morning Misti greets Joelle at the hedge in a frantic state.

"Where were you yesterday? I waited and waited, but you didn't come out. I knocked on the door, but no one answered. I had to run to school, and I was late."

"I said you shouldn't wait for me every day!" Joelle snaps at her, stricken with guilt.

"Where were you? I didn't know where you were!"

"I was somewhere else," Joelle tells her angrily. "You shouldn't depend on me so much. I can't always walk with you for the rest of your life!"

The truth is, Joelle forgot about her. In the excitement of cutting school and going to the Crying Rocks with Carlos, she forgot how Misti would come and stand behind the hedge in the cold, gazing at her door. Joelle can't apologize, though. If she apologized, it would mean she was taking responsibility for Misti, and she doesn't want it. She can't bear even the thought of such a burden.

"You need to grow up and take care of your own problems," Joelle finds herself saying in a hard voice.

"What problems?" Misti can barely answer. The glinty sheen of Joelle's beer-tab necklace is just visible around her neck, under her winter coat.

"Penny Perrino, the Secret Princesses who don't like you, I don't know. All your stuff. It's not my job."

"But I only want to walk with you," Misti says in a tremulous voice. Her eyes suddenly bulge with tears. With a great sniff, she tries to hold them back, but unsuccessfully. They overflow onto her cheeks.

"I was scared when you didn't come out," Misti explains, weeping. "I thought you didn't like me!"

There is a long silence, punctuated by the sound of their shoes crunching along the frozen sidewalk. Overnight the light snow has turned to ice. Puddles have become congealed craters of crystal.

Somewhere along their route Joelle realizes that her arm has reached out and gone around Misti's shoulders. She can't help it, she feels compelled to care about this small girl. She can't push her away or let her down, and inside the circle of Joelle's arm Misti knows it. As they trudge on down the street she gazes up from time to time into Joelle's face, not speaking until the elementary school comes into view.

"Bye," Misti says at the turn to the front walk. She detaches herself lightly from Joelle's arm and trots away.

"See you," Joelle replies.

Somehow everything has been fixed. Tomorrow Misti will be waiting outside her house, as usual, and Joelle won't mind. Secretly, she'll be happy. Misti has found a place in her that, mysteriously and inexplicably, needed filling.

11

ONE MORNING A FEW DAYS LATER JOELLE
is called out of her first period class and told
to go to the principal's office.

She's quite sure this has to do with her cutting school and expects to see Carlos herded
in beside her. The school has detected the
forgery in their absence notes. Or perhaps
someone did see them, as Carlos had worried, in a place where they shouldn't have
been that day. Whatever, Joelle needs a few
minutes to martial her defense before turning herself in, and she takes a short detour
into the girls' bathroom.

There she decides to use Aunt Mary
Louise's bad health for her excuse. Carlos
will have to fend for himself. She stayed
home to watch over Aunt Mary Louise, she'll

say, and forged her own note so Aunt Mary Louise wouldn't be bothered. Joelle will claim she was scared that "something might happen" to her aunt that day. You can argue scared feelings and get away with it. Besides, it's not a complete lie. She really is worried about Aunt Mary Louise and lately has been going upstairs to check on her before leaving. Aunt Mary Louise has scoffed at this new show of concern, of course.

"Get out of my sight!" she'd told Joelle yesterday with a half smile. "Can't a person have any privacy?"

"You can't if you're going to fall over and knock yourself stupid," Joelle had said. There have been other dizzy spells since the one reported to Carlos.

"If I'm going to do that, I'll let you know," Aunt Mary Louise had replied. "Don't worry, you'll be the first to know."

It's their usual game. If Joelle has learned anything from Aunt Mary Louise, it's how to joke around when you want to cover something up.

When she finally walks into the school office, Joelle is primed and ready to defend herself, but from the first minute, she sees that something else is going on. The secretaries keep glancing over with sympathetic smiles as she sits, waiting for Mrs. Lincoln, the principal, to call her in. One secretary even offers her a cup of water. Joelle says, "No, thanks," and glares at her.

When Mrs. Lincoln appears, she doesn't ask Joelle into her office. With an arm around Joelle's back, she guides her out to the hall, where they walk toward the front entrance of the school.

"Honey, there's been an accident at home," she says with such terrible kindness in her voice that Joelle's heart takes a leap and begins to pump. "Your aunt has gone to the hospital. Now, don't worry. Someone will be here to pick you up in a few minutes. You don't have to come back today if it's not possible."

"What happened?"

"I think your family can tell you better than I. They'll know the details."

"What details?" Joelle exclaims. "Did Aunt Mary Louise fall?"

"I think so," Mrs. Lincoln says. "I believe she did." Her forehead is wrinkled with concern. Her arm squeezes Joelle's shoulder, then drops off as they approach the door. "Let's just wait here a moment. I understand someone's on the way."

Almost instantly, Vernon's pickup appears across the parking lot and rattles toward them. This is such an odd sight that Joelle forgets for a minute to be frightened. Vernon has, literally, never been on the school grounds. He's always at work. Joelle wonders if it really could be him driving or if someone has stolen his truck. Is it a trick?

But when the pickup pulls closer, she sees Vernon's slouching bulk through the windshield. Mrs. Lincoln gives her shoulder another irritating squeeze before Joelle can fend her off. Then the truck pulls up, and she's getting in.

"What's going on?" she finds herself shouting. "Why are you here?" And Vernon, being who he is, doesn't answer. He puts the truck in gear, steps on the gas, and starts off without even looking at her.

"Where are we going?" Joelle yells, though she already guesses where. They are pulling onto the main road, heading out of Marshfield toward the highway. The hospital is in Westerly, a few exits down. She's been there herself, for stitches one time when she cut her foot on a piece of glass. Vernon is trying for every bit of power in the old pickup. His messy turkey-farm boot is hard down, grinding the accelerator into the mat.

"She called Emergency. She couldn't breathe," he says, speaking for the first time as they pass a car. "They came and got her."

"When? I was just there!" It's only nine thirty in the morning. "She was okay when I left, just getting up. What happened?" Joelle asks, remembering how she'd planned her silly lie about Aunt Mary Louise. Now, in a most frightening way, the lie has come to life.

"I don't know. I don't know," Vernon mutters. He mops his big hand over his face and hunches toward the windshield.

Sometime later, as they're entering the hospital parking lot, he begins to pound his fist against the steering wheel.

"What?" Joelle cries.

"She wouldn't see a doctor," he chokes out. "I told her to go, but she wouldn't. I should have made her. I should have taken her there myself."

"You didn't know she was this sick," Joelle says.

"Yes, I did! I knew!"

They park and race on foot for the entrance that says EMERGENCY PATIENTS ONLY. When they get inside, Vernon talks to someone in a glass booth. He goes off with a nurse, so Joelle finds a chair, but she immediately has to stand up again and walk around to keep her stomach down. It's rising, threatening to turn over. To calm herself, she tries to think back to what Aunt Mary Louise looked like when she left this morning. She was on her feet, making the usual remarks. It was going to be "Italian night" that evening, she'd announced. Joelle was supposed to pick up some dry pasta and French bread on the way home.

"You want French bread for Italian night?" Joelle had kidded her.

"Well, what's the difference? There's no difference that I can ever tell."

And Joelle had explained that French bread was long and skinny while Italian bread was short and fat, and that there was a tremendous difference to people who knew bread.

"I'm not one of those!" Aunt Mary Louise had declared cheerfully. "All I know is how to make a good American tomato sauce, which I'm going to pass on to you tonight. It'll come in handy someday when you get hitched."

This was another joke between them. "Getting hitched" is Aunt Mary Louise's phrase for getting married, which, as she's well aware, is positively the last item on Joelle's list of things to do.

Suddenly, Vernon is back. He wanders out into the waiting room and looks vaguely around for her. Joelle is beside him in a flash.

"Where is she? Can I see her?"

He shakes his head.

"Why not? How is she?"

"She's gone," Vernon tells her in a bewildered voice.

"Gone! Where?"

Vernon waves a hand, aimlessly. He looks over at the glassed-in office where a nurse hovers, shuffling a pile of documents.

"Just . . . gone," he repeats. Everything in his face is sagging. The whites of his eyes have turned pink.

Joelle stands very still. She stares at him and tries not to understand what this means.

"Where did they take her?" she asks in a dumb voice.

"Not yet," Vernon answers, just as dumbly. "I have to sign some papers first." He wanders toward the nurse behind the glass.

"Are you all right?" Joelle hears her ask him. "Can we give you something? The doctor will be here in a minute to explain. I know it must be a shock for you."

Since he apparently has to fill out and sign a large number of forms, she kindly invites him to come in and use an empty seat in her office.

"Is this your daughter?" Joelle hears the nurse ask.

And Vernon answers, "Yes, it is."

"She can come in too."

"She says you can come in too," Vernon turns and tells Joelle, as if he's translating from a foreign language. And it might as well be, because Joelle can't understand one thing that's going on. She's standing and staring at the nurse in the glassed-in office and at the papers that need to be signed and at Vernon, who has just called her his daughter. And nothing is real. It's like a dream you half wake from in the middle of the night and it's too bizarre to even try to figure out.

"Come in, dear," Joelle hears the nurse say again. "You can sit over there."

12

EVERYONE IS SHOCKED BY AUNT MARY Louise dying so suddenly. No one had expected that she was remotely close to the end—not her friends in town or her former co-workers at the chicken plant. Not even the Tiverton relatives, who haven't set eyes on her in years but still claim her as one of them, it seems. On the eve of Aunt Mary Louise's funeral day they appear at the front door without warning, six of them, bearing food, flowers, and God's love at full strength. Jesus is watching, they assure Joelle. He has taken Aunt Mary Louise to His heavenly mansion and will tell Joelle what to do next . . . if she will only listen.

Vernon would have shut the door in their faces, but he's back working at the turkey farm. Joelle invites them in—they are another chapter in the dream she is dreaming—and seats them in the living room, as Aunt Mary Louise would have done, she feels sure. Despite the passage of time, she recognizes them: sisters, brothers, a heavily bearded cousin. They resemble Aunt Mary Louise in creepy, distorted ways; all are marshmallow pale and small of stature, as she was. Joelle towers darkly above them, repeating words the doctor used when he spoke to her and Vernon on that unreal morning in the hospital.

Stress. Smoking. Overweight. Congestion. Lungs. Heart attack.

The relatives listen with closed faces. They watch Joelle, suspiciously. Maybe they think she's trying to pull another fast one on them, the way she did when she reached for the corn bread too soon.

"The family would like a chance to make a final statement at the service," one brother informs her, as if Aunt Mary Louise has been kidnapped all these years and her body is only now being returned.

At the service arranged by Vernon at a local funeral parlor the next afternoon, quite a few mourners come by to pay their respects. They approach and speak softly to Joelle, reaching out to hug her or grasp her hand. They stand in line and file past the gleaming wood coffin where Aunt Mary Louise lies, weirdly waxen, in a slate-blue outfit the funeral home put on her. It's a dress and jacket she hasn't worn in all the years Joelle has known her. Vernon chose it from her closet, probably recognizing it from some far-off era when they'd first been together.

Vernon looks terrible. He sits slumped in a folding chair, not even trying to greet visitors. A subtle atmosphere of menace drifts off him—off the boots he hasn't bothered to change from this morning's stint at the turkey ranch, off his hunched back and the beefy hands cupped over his knees. Not once does he go up to file by Aunt Mary Louise, and only a few people venture over to speak to him. Most don't seem to know him. They are Aunt Mary Louise's friends. Joelle suspects that he hasn't told his own group about what's happened, the men he drinks with at night and works with during the day. That would be like him, to hole up and bury any outward sign of feeling.

In the week since Aunt Mary Louise died, he's hardly spoken to Joelle. But he's stayed home in the evenings with her, cooked dinner, helped wash up, watched television beside her on the couch. While others may feel afraid of his sullen slouch (the Tiverton relatives won't go anywhere near him), Joelle, for once, is not. Underneath that threatening surface, she perceives his pain. When, at the end of the service proper, Aunt Mary Louise's brother rises to speak the final words ("Though she was a poor sinner in life, departing from Thy divine guidance, yet by her death Thou makest her acceptable in Thine eyes . . ."), she sees Vernon clench the chair in fury to keep from coming out of it, while at the same time a river of tears pours silently down his face.

The afternoon is nearly over and the Tiverton relatives have departed (taking with them most of the flowers they'd originally brought) when Carlos comes awkwardly into the room. He's dressed in a dark suit and tie and looks so completely out of place that Joelle is embarrassed. She turns her head away and pretends not to see him. He spots her, though, and comes over.

"Hello, Joelle. I'm so sorry about your aunt," he says.

"Well, it's a free country. You didn't need to come," she snaps back. It's what she's wanted to shout at every person who's said this same stupid thing to her all afternoon. Politeness has kept her numb. But with Carlos she doesn't need to be polite. "So go home," she tells him. "You can go home now."

"That's okay. I want to stay."

"Well, she's over there." Joelle jabs a crude thumb toward Aunt Mary Louise's box.

"I know."

"They put makeup on her."

"Makeup?"

"To make her look, you know, alive!"

This is such an over-the-top remark that a big lump comes into her throat and she almost starts laughing. Carlos gazes at her.

"Can I sit down?"

Joelle nods. Her hand is over her mouth. She's afraid she really will start laughing. Luckily, he's distracted by the scene around them and she has time to get herself together.

"How've you been?" she inquires after a while.

"Okay. Everybody at school feels bad for you."

"Oh, sure," Joelle says. She hasn't gone to school all week. She's stayed home reading and watching TV. Except for short conversations with Misti, who stops by in the mornings as usual, she hasn't seen anyone.

"When are you coming back?" Carlos asks.

"Monday. Otherwise, they'd probably arrest me."

Carlos is looking at her. She knows what he's thinking—that she doesn't seem that sad. She's wondered about it herself. She hasn't cried once.

"What about you?" Joelle asks him.

"Me?" He gazes at her.

"Did you tell your parents that you know about Daniel yet?"

"No," he says in a defensive voice.

"How about the skull? Did you tell your dad we found it?"

"You don't want to talk about that now," he says, glancing around the gloomy room.

A disturbance has broken out at the door. Some other latecomers are arriving, a group of tall, dark-skinned men with slicked-back, black hair. Though two ushers, perhaps alarmed by their looks, try to stop them for questioning, they break away and walk directly over to Vernon, who springs up to shake their hands.

"Actually, I did tell my father about it," Carlos says in Joelle's ear. "He asked if I'd made it to the rocks, so we got on the subject." He leans toward her. "I showed him how the skull fit in my hand. He said it might have been a child's, because it was so small."

"So the Crying Rocks was the scene of a massacre," Joelle says, keeping her eye on the dark men. She finds them familiar in a way she can't identify.

"We'd have to excavate more bones to be sure."

"Did you tell him about the cries we heard?"

Carlos shakes his head. "He would think I was crazy."

"Do you think we were?" She turns to look at him.

"No. We heard something. I keep thinking about that."

"I do too." With a nod toward Vernon's visitors, she adds, "Who are those guys?"

Carlos examines them and shrugs. "I've

never seen them before. They look like brothers."

There are five. Everyone is talking. One man leans forward and clasps Vernon around his shoulders. Others touch his arms and pat his back. Vernon's head is down, accepting their expressions of sympathy as he has no one else's. All of a sudden, he looks up and points his finger straight at Joelle, and the group turns to stare at her. She glances away fast.

Beside her Carlos's chair squeaks. "I wasn't going to say this right now, because you must already be pretty upset about everything, but . . ."

"What?"

"It's probably not a good time. . . ."

"You can tell me. I'm fine," Joelle exclaims.

"Okay." Carlos lowers his voice again. "My father told me why he was looking for bones underneath the rocks, by the swamp. There's another, older story about the reason the rocks cry. It doesn't have anything to do with the English or the massacre or mothers trying to save their children. It's an Indian story."

"Tell!"

"They left their babies there, the ones they didn't want."

"What?"

"Children who had some deformity or were born too sick to take care of. Indian women brought them there. That's the legend that's come down, my father said. Some stories say they threw them off the rocks into the swamp. There's supposed to be this buildup of little skeletons below. My father was trying to find out if it was true."

"But that's . . . that's terrible!"

"Life was hard back then, my father said. A tribe's survival depended on the health of its members. There was no place for weakness. Remember what we read? The early settlers saw only perfect children."

Joelle stares at him. His words have caught her off guard. They've found a crack in a wall that has long been sealed. Now, a memory is attempting to snake its way through. Far off she hears noise—shouting, pounding, the shriek of a window being raised.

She blocks it out.

"That isn't right," she tells Carlos angrily.

"The Narragansetts weren't savages. They were civilized people with a special love of children. We read that, too."

"I know, but—"

"The Pilgrims said they spoiled their children," Joelle goes on. "There's no way they could . . . I mean, how could they? How could anyone do that to . . ."

She can't speak anymore or she will cry. The tears are just inside, trying to burst out. She won't let them. She will not. She shuts her eyes hard and makes her mind dark, impenetrable.

Beside her she hears Carlos's voice say, "Joelle? Are you okay? I knew it wasn't a good time for this. Joelle?" But she can't answer. After a long while, she feels a hand on her shoulder, and when she opens her eyes, a man is standing in front of her. It's an usher who has come across the room to say that, regretfully, time is running short.

"What time?" Joelle asks. Turning her head, she's surprised to see that Aunt Mary Louise's casket is being removed from the room. The usher nods apologetically. The funereal urn will be ready to be picked up tomorrow. If they would be so kind . . . another service scheduled . . . a busy season . . . so very sorry.

"You better go," Carlos says.

"Not yet! That story your father told you . . ."

"We can talk about it later."

"When?"

"Listen, Joelle. You need to rest after all this."

"Rest! You must be kidding! I've *been* resting. All week. I can't stand resting anymore."

Carlos is gazing at her uneasily. This is not how someone acts who has just lost the most-loved person in her life, he is probably thinking. She is supposed to be sniffling, not arguing about early Indian tribal practices. Her heart is supposed to be broken. Nothing is broken inside Joelle. Her anger has returned full-force. She is dry-eyed and furious.

"Come on," she says, "let's finish this somewhere else."

"I can't. My mother dropped me off. She's coming back to get me in a few minutes, then we're going to meet my father."

Joelle glares at him. "Okay then, tonight. After dinner. I'll meet you at the park. I'd ask you to my house, but . . ." She glances in the direction of Vernon, who is now standing by the door, waiting for her. His tall, dark visitors are gone, and he is glowering at everyone again.

"I'm sorry, I can't," Carlos says.

"Why not?"

"We're driving to Boston for the weekend." He looks at her unhappily, then admits: "It's my mother's birthday, I'm really sorry."

"Why are you sorry?"

"Well, because it's a bad time for my mother to have a birthday, just when your mother, I mean your aunt . . . Anyway, I know you're sad and probably want to—"

"No, I don't!" Joelle shouts.

"I'll call you when we get back."

"Forget it."

"That will give you some time to—"

"Listen, will you stop talking to me that way? I can't stand that kind of nice talk right now. It makes me sick, in fact. And don't tell me what's better for me because you don't know."

"You're right, I don't," Carlos agrees. "I'm really—"

"And if you say you're sorry one more time, I'll strangle you!" Joelle screams at him.

Before he can bleat out another word of sympathy, she jumps up and runs to join Vernon at the door.

———————

"Who were those men who came in at the end?" she asks after they arrive home that afternoon.

Vernon doesn't answer at first. He's got the refrigerator open and is staring inside, as if he's looking for something but can't remember what. He closes the door and stands in front of it, empty-handed. His face is stubbly and tired-looking.

"Friends," he mutters. "Old friends."

"From where?"

"The railroad, when I worked there."

"I never saw them before."

"They live in different places now."

"That was nice of them to come. I guess you haven't seen them lately?"

"We get together sometimes. You want to go out to eat?"

"I'm not that hungry yet," Joelle says.

"Later, then." Vernon heads for the back

door and is almost outside when he stops and turns around. Joelle can guess why—he forgot to tell her where he's going. It's something new he's started, keeping her informed of his movements. Before, with Aunt Mary Louise, he went wherever he went without a word of explanation. She could never be sure of his plans. Joelle doesn't know if he's changed as a kindness to her or if he just wants to reassure himself that she'll be there when he comes back.

"I've got chicks hatching soon. I'm going out to check the shed," he says to her now. "I'll be a half hour or so. Then maybe we'll be hungry."

"Okay."

But still he doesn't leave. He hesitates at the door, staring into the yard. When he turns around to look at her again, she knows he has something to get off his chest.

"They're Indians," he says. "Could you see that?"

"I guess I could," Joelle finds herself answering.

"I'll tell you about them sometime."

"Okay."

"They're good people."

"They looked good," Joelle says. "Tall."

"We used to go to the ball games together, up in Pawtucket. Sometimes up to Boston. I loved Mary Louise, though. For all that, I loved her."

Joelle nods. "I know."

"That's about it," Vernon says. "I'll check the eggs now."

"See you later."

After he's gone, Joelle reviews this weird conversation and comes to the conclusion that Vernon was confessing to her something he never told Aunt Mary Louise. What it could be, she can't guess, though a strange idea now lurks at the edge her mind. She thinks back to the Indian men at the funeral parlor, long-legged and handsome, enclosing Vernon in a sympathetic ring of dark suits. She watches again as their heads, following Vernon's finger, swing eagerly around to find her.

13

A *DULLNESS SETTLES OVER JOELLE IN THE* weeks after the funeral. Her anger drains away, and for a while it seems possible to imagine that Aunt Mary Louise is only temporarily out of sight. School absorbs the better part of her waking hours with its daily rigor of classes and labs, assignments and tests. Outside the weather is wintry. December arrives, Christmas vacation comes and goes. Temperatures hover in the teens and twenties; ice and snow are controlling principles.

Under the circumstances, there seems no point in discussing hikes in the forest or old Native American folklore. Carlos, after a few attempts at conversation in the hall, now passes her without comment. She's made it clear she doesn't want to talk to him. Her beaded headband has been retired, and she's stopped braiding her hair. (Misti and the Secret Princesses have followed suit.)

The Narragansetts are far away in the seventeenth century, taking cover from their own winter in forested valleys that no longer exist, making hunting forays along trails now sealed with asphalt. They are speaking to one another in a lost language about a way of life that will shortly be erased and, soon after that, forgotten. Or worse, Joelle thinks, it will be dug up, misunderstood, and falsely reconstructed by descendants of their white conquerors. For this is certainly what has happened with the murderous story Carlos's father told him about the Crying Rocks. How could such a story be true? Joelle thinks about the small skull she unearthed at the swamp. She thinks about the crack in its forehead. No, she won't believe that such things ever happened.

When the natives bury their dead, she reads one afternoon at home, inadvertently, in an overdue library book about Narragansett Indian life, *they sew up the corpse in a mat and so put it in the earth. If the party be a sachem, they cover him with many curious mats and bury all his riches with him. If it be a child, the father will also put his own most special jewels and ornaments in the earth with it. If it be the man or woman of the house, they will pull down the mats and leave the house frame standing, and bury them in or near the same, and wither remove their dwelling or give over housekeeping.* —EDWARD WINSLOW, 1623

This passage comes closer to echoing her own feelings about Aunt Mary Louise's death than anything else Joelle has heard or read. Briefly, she considers asking Vernon if they can "remove their dwelling" too, to another house where Aunt Mary Louise is not always about to enter the kitchen. But, of course, this is not practical. For one thing, Vernon's chick business is booming.

The first batch of chicks hatched and sold at a good price a couple of days after Aunt Mary Louise's funeral. By the beginning of January the second batch is ready, and this one, too, finds an interested buyer. The big chicken farms are thriving. Steak has been associated with heart disease and clogged arteries. Chicken is the healthy meat of choice. But raising chicks from the egg is a time-consuming business, one better farmed out to independent suppliers like Vernon.

"I'm doing okay with this," he tells Joelle one night at dinner, amazement in his voice. Somehow it's March now. "I'm onto my fourth batch of chicks with no problems," he declares. "No problems at all! I keep waiting for what's going to go wrong."

"Why would anything go wrong?" Joelle asks.

"Because it usually does," Vernon answers in a resigned voice. "The only thing I ever did good was marry your Aunt Mary Louise, and look what happened to that."

Joelle lowers her head and keeps eating. They don't talk about her much, but Aunt Mary Louise is always on their minds.

"She was the one brought me luck," Vernon goes on.

"You didn't look that happy about your luck when she was here," says Joelle, remembering their fights.

"Just in the last year or so, I was worrying, that's why," Vernon says. "After she had to quit work, I was trying to think of how to make it so she wouldn't ever have to go back.

Finally, I hit on it, and see what happens? It's too late for her."

Vernon shakes his head and gets up from the table. "That's bad luck," he tells Joelle from the kitchen. "So I'm waiting for what's next."

"I think that's a stupid way to look at things," Joelle tells him. "If you believe something's going to go wrong, it probably will just from you setting yourself up for it. Besides, I thought you had backers. Wouldn't they help out if you got into trouble?"

Vernon's large form appears in the kitchen door. "How'd you know that?"

"What?"

"About my backers?"

"I heard you talking."

"When? To who?"

"To Aunt Mary Louise." She looks at him. "You were talking in the night, and I woke up."

"That was none of your business," he says roughly.

"I heard some other things, too," Joelle goes on, staring straight at him. "I heard you had secrets you kept from her, and she knew you were lying to her and felt bad."

Vernon turns on his heel after this and

does some washing up at the sink. There's a lot of dish clanking and the sound of the fridge opening and slamming shut about five times. Joelle stays where she is at the table. Even on good evenings, she and Vernon don't fit in the kitchen together. They get in each other's way. With Aunt Mary Louise, it was different. She and Joelle knew each other's moves, how to kind of dance around one another. The work was done fast and well, with a lot of joking and nobody's feelings being stepped on.

Joelle leans over the table and lays her head on her arms. It's funny how you miss people, she thinks, how remembering a little thing like moves in the kitchen can bring back the whole person and make you ache to be with them. You begin to want them so much that sometimes you see them or hear them, walking ahead along the street, talking in a nearby room. It's your imagination, of course, but in that second, you catch your breath and wonder if . . .

Vernon appears in the doorway. "I'm going out."

"Okay."

"Will you be all right?"

"Of course. What do you expect?"

"I've got some folks to see. I'll be back late. You go on to bed."

"I'll go when I'm ready."

Vernon puts on his coat and gazes at her. "Should I tell you where I'll be?" he asks.

"Why?" says Joelle. "You're coming back, aren't you?"

He lowers his head and walks out the door.

One Saturday evening not long after, Joelle calls Carlos at home. She's not particularly eager to talk to him, but dinner is long over. Vernon has gone off again. He's been out every night all week, meeting friends, he says, leaving her alone in the house. Suddenly, she doesn't want to be alone anymore.

"Want to come out for a while?" she asks when Carlos answers the phone.

"Right now? It's eleven o'clock!"

"No, next week," Joelle snaps. Then, hearing him draw an irritated breath, she makes amends. "Sorry. I didn't mean that."

"Where were you thinking of going?" he inquires cautiously. They haven't really talked for months, just a distant "hello" or snipped-off "hi" when their paths cross between classes. It's strange because, better than anyone else at school, they know each other's thoughts. Joelle knows that Carlos has the guilty weight of Daniel's cries on his conscience and still cannot tell his parents. Carlos knows that Joelle is struggling to go on without Aunt Mary Louise, though she rejects all offers of sympathy with disdain.

"How about the park?" Joelle suggests. "It's a really clear night. We could look for constellations. Did you read that part about the Narragansetts? Even the youngest children could name the stars. They didn't have the same names the English had, but they knew their patterns and how they moved. Maybe it was like TV back then. You'd settle down in some dark field and watch after dinner."

"High drama," Carlos says sarcastically.

"It might be fun."

March is well along by now. The last snow has melted, though the weather is still chilly.

A faint scent of spring fills the crisp morning air during Joelle's walks with Misti to school. In yards along their way the first crocuses' purple and yellow beaks have pushed through the grass. By afternoon, temperatures are warm enough for the Secret Princess Club to be out and about again, though lately, their awe over Joelle's royal status seems to have diminished. Not content to just follow, they've taken to yelling at her, under Penny Perrino's direction.

"Hey, look over here!"

"Can't you even speak English?"

"Where's your tiara? Did you leave your jewels at home?"

Misti has long been banned from their meetings.

On the telephone Carlos is apparently trying to decide whether he'll come out or not. "Well . . . ," he says finally.

"You don't have to. I'd understand," Joelle says.

"It's not that. I want to, but . . ."

"Your *padre y madre* are on guard, no? They no like you to leave," Joelle says in a thick Spanish accent that makes him laugh.

"Yeah. I mean, *si.*"

"Well, make a getaway down the drain-pipe or something. They'll never know. They probably—"

"Did it when they were young. I know."

"Well, they probably did."

"Okay. Give me a half hour. I'll try making a break for it. If I'm not there in forty-five minutes . . ."

"I'll notify the morgue."

"The morgue!"

"To let them know you'll be arriving shortly. S.T.T.E."

"What's S.T.T.E.?"

"Shot Trying to Escape."

"Oh, thanks. That gives me confidence."

They both have a morbid chuckle over this and hang up.

The night is cold and blazing with stars when Joelle steps out into it twenty minutes later. The streets are dark, lit only by occasional passing headlights or, behind fences and hedges, the glow of individual homes. As she approaches the park, however, streetlamps illuminate the sidewalk, and around a corner, adjacent to the old barbecue pit, she spots the familiar rusty red dome of a VW Bug. A campfire's flickering glow comes through the trees. Queenie is there, cooking a late dinner for herself, apparently. The smoky-sweet smell of grilled meat wafts into Joelle's nostrils, and before she can stop herself, she's heading over in that direction.

"Pssst!" Carlos flags her down from behind a scraggly bush.

"Hey, Tonto! You made it. Any bullet wounds?" She feels amazingly happy to see him.

He grins. "It was easy. My parents were watching *Invasion of the Body Snatchers* on video."

"That'll paralyze them for hours."

"If you can believe it, they were asleep!"

They both laugh. It's good to be together again. The late-night air gives off a wildness that makes Joelle feel almost delirious.

"What's going on over there?" She points toward the barbecue pit.

"Hamburgers, from the smell. Want to take a look?"

"Absolutely."

They sneak up on the fire, which casts a merry glow on nearby trees. Queenie is crouched over the flames, a stick in each hand, prodding two mounds of meat on a tiny grill. Her face is ruddy and alert with interest. Between the crackles of fire, Joelle hears her humming loudly to herself a private melody that seems to have no beginning or end. Though her clothes are grubby and her hair falls over her face in an untamed curtain of grayish black, she appears thoroughly contented, as fully at home in this wall-less, roofless place as any inhabitant of Marshfield's surrounding houses. Watching her, Joelle is filled with a longing to join her there by her cozy fire. After a minute or so, though, Carlos grows impatient.

"Come on," he whispers. "I'm freezing standing here. Let's walk around."

"Just a little longer," Joelle whispers back. "I want to see what she does next."

Her meat lumps cooked, Queenie deftly scrapes them onto a flat square plate that may be no more than a discarded house shingle. She rifles in a plastic bag at her side for a piece of sliced bread and, wrapping the bread around the meat, begins to eat hungrily, still sitting in her crouch beside the fire.

It's at this point that Carlos, shifting his weight restlessly from one leg to another, loses his balance and stumbles a bit, cracking the twigs beneath his shoes.

Instantly, Queenie's head comes up and she is on her feet, her sharp eyes probing the night. She leaves her dinner on the ground and, without a word, walks swiftly toward their hiding place. In a short few seconds (or gasps, in Joelle's case) she has discovered them and is pushing aside the thin arms of the bush they're cowering behind. She stares at them, her dark glance moving from face to face. Then, as if they are of no more interest than some predictable woodland phenomenon—a pair of rabbits out of their hole or two old tree stumps—she releases the branches and trudges back without comment to her campfire. There she nestles down in her previous spot, takes up her food, and continues to eat, not bothering to look at them again.

Two minutes later, her supper finished, she lights the stub end of an already well-smoked cigar and, rocking slowly back and forth, begins her loud humming song again. Joelle touches Carlos's arm.

"I want to talk to her," she whispers. "Do you think she'd let us?"

Carlos shakes his head. "She's too crazy."

"How do you know? Have you ever tried?"

"She won't talk. She'll run away. That's why she's out here, to get away from people."

"She didn't run away when she saw us."

"She probably thought we were statues. Who knows what she thought?"

"I'm going to try," Joelle whispers. "Will you wait for me? I might need some backup."

When Carlos reluctantly nods, she steps around the bush and begins to walk slowly toward the fire.

14

QUEENIE GLANCES UP IN ALARM AS Joelle comes toward her through the trees. Her body tenses, ready for flight. But when Joelle stops on the other side of the fire and sits down cross-legged, she resumes her place, though her eyes follow Joelle's every movement.

Joelle doesn't speak to her. Instinct tells her to keep silent. She allows several minutes to pass, leaning occasionally toward the fire to nudge a wayward piece of wood into a better position. She feels Carlos's steady gaze on her back.

Across the fire Queenie smokes her cigar stub and examines her visitor. Joelle lowers her head and allows her to look, unchallenged. She's comfortable sitting by this fire, stars overhead, cold breath of night on her cheeks. She feels as if she's been here before, and she's not surprised when Queenie clears her throat and, half rising from her crouch, turns and spits on the ground behind. This, too, seems familiar in a distant way.

"Thanks for letting me sit here," Joelle says.

Queenie looks at her and says nothing.

"I'm Joelle. You're Queenie, right? You know how to make a good fire," Joelle tells her. "You must camp out a lot."

Queenie puffs her cigar.

"You go into the woods sometimes too. I've seen your car over there by the North–South Trail."

She's just talking, trying to make conversation, but at the mention of the trail Queenie responds. She smiles.

"My friend Carlos and I have been hiking there," Joelle continues. "You know, my friend who's back in the bushes? You saw him just now, right?"

Queenie's smile fades. "I know you," she says gravely. "I've been watching you for a long time. You won't tell, will you?"

"That you're camping here? No, of course

not. My friend won't either. Is it all right if he sits with us? It's cold where he is."

Queenie says nothing, but she doesn't protest, so Joelle stands up and calls to Carlos, and he comes and sits by the fire. When Queenie eyes him warily, as if she might be thinking of bolting, Joelle tries to distract her with more conversation.

"Somebody said you're a descendant of Indians who used to live around here. We've been studying the Narragansetts. Were those your people?"

Queenie's dark eyes come back to her. After a moment she takes the cigar out of her mouth and smiles again. Her teeth are yellowed with tobacco stain. "My people were kings and queens. That is what they say, kings and queens. Do you remember that I know you?" she asks.

"From the library?" Joelle guesses. "That's right, we passed in the library. That's where my friend and I have been doing our research. We're interested in what happened to the Native American tribes around here. There's a place out in the forest called the Crying Rocks. Have you ever heard of it?"

At the mention of the Crying Rocks,

Queenie's smile vanishes. She glances over her shoulder, then back at Joelle and Carlos.

"That is a sad place," she whispers. "Don't go."

"Why?" Joelle asks. "What have you heard about it? Was there a massacre there?"

Queenie shakes her head. "Sad," she repeats. "Many ghosts and spirits live there. People who go come back scared. They can't speak of the sadness they feel. And some do not come back."

Carlos glances up. "What do you mean?" he asks sharply.

Queenie grasps one of her cooking sticks and probes the fire. A fresh blaze springs up, lighting the flat, broad planes of her brown face. Leaning closer to the fire, she begins her slow rocking motion, the one that accompanied her humming before.

"Can you tell us a little more?" Joelle asks her. "Please. We'd like to know."

With her eyes on the fire, Queenie keeps rocking and rocking. Once again she makes the fire leap with her stick. Then she begins to speak in the same humming drone as before when she sang her song.

"If you go near this place, the Crying Rocks,

you will hear them, the baby ghosts: Woo-woo! Woo-woo! The mother ghosts: Scree-scree! They make these sounds, and many others. Some say, 'Oh, that is the wind,' but they are wrong."

"So what is it?" Carlos asks.

"Ghosts, like I said."

"Yes, but why are the ghosts there?"

Queenie draws herself up and stares off into the dark. "Never you mind."

"Is it true that, long ago, Indian children born sick or crippled were abandoned there?" Carlos asks straight out. "My father heard that. He said there are other places like this, that many ancient cultures had them, in many parts of the world. They've come down to us as weeping bogs or wailing cliffs. Ghosts are guilty consciences, he says."

"Carlos, be quiet!" Joelle murmurs.

Queenie is glaring at him too. "A ghost is a ghost," she tells him. "It is real and can do what it wants."

"Then how—," Carlos begins, but Queenie cuts him off.

"The story of the Crying Rocks is for our people, not for you," she tells him angrily. "Only our women can tell their daughters.

Only we can understand. Isn't it so?" She looks around with bright eyes at Joelle. "Do you remember?" she asks. "It is your story too."

"Remember what?" Joelle replies. "That was hundreds of years ago."

"Listen—," Carlos starts to protest. Maybe he wants to bring up his one-sixteenth Indian blood, or maybe he's going to point out that the Crying Rocks story is no longer a private Narragansett legend. It's gone out into the world and joined up with other stories from human history. Its events can be proved or disproved by the excavation of real bones. Whatever Carlos intends to say, Joelle lays her hand on his arm to stop him.

"Don't. You'll upset her."

And he stops. They all sit still, watching the fire jump and spark. In the distance several cars can be heard passing on the street. From overhead, the roar of an airliner crossing the sky drifts down to them. As it fades Joelle feels the shimmy of a memory. Glancing at Queenie, she is suddenly aware of another fire, one that burned long ago and far away, so far away that it was lost all this time and she's just now caught sight of its flames through the dark.

The air was chilly then, as it is now. The fire was well made and warm. The sound in the distance was not of cars on a street or a plane in the sky. It came from train wheels speeding along a track. *Clackety-clackety-clackety,* the train races past Joelle and fades out of sight into the night.

She turns to Queenie and says, "I do remember now. I know you, too. You were my friend, weren't you? We cooked out . . . somewhere. Where was that?"

Queenie smiles her wide tobacco-stained smile.

"I've been watching you," she says proudly. "We've all been watching you. But, shush! We must not speak."

"People have been watching me?" Joelle says.

Beside her Carlos leans forward with interest.

"What people?" he asks, but Queenie presses a finger to her mouth and shakes her head.

"I promised," she says to Joelle. "We all promised. You won't tell on me, will you? You were so little then. Now you're big and look like her."

"Who?" Joelle says, barely breathing.

"Like Sylvie," Queenie says. "She was very tall, like you."

———————

It's past 1:00 A.M. and Vernon is already home when Joelle lets herself into the kitchen through the back door. The house lights are all out. At the top of the stairs she hears heavy breathing coming from Vernon's room and guesses he never noticed she was gone. It's not his habit to check up on her. Aunt Mary Louise was the person who looked in, to close a window or pick her clothes off the floor. One of the changes Joelle has had to get used to is that Vernon doesn't intrude on her this way. He's made no attempt to take Aunt Mary Louise's place, and maybe it's just as well. Joelle isn't sure she needs that kind of attention anymore.

When she gets in bed, she can't sleep at first. Queenie's campfire burns in her brain, and whether she wants to or not, she finds herself groping for other memories to connect to the amazing facts unearthed tonight.

"You had a nice bed. A box like a house," Queenie had said when Joelle asked her about the depot. But "I don't allow no dogs near me," she'd announced, so perhaps the little dog and the story of the shared Snickers bar were Joelle's own inventions.

"They brought you in by a freight train, scared they were going to get caught," Queenie said.

"Who?" Joelle demanded, and Queenie wouldn't tell. She shook her head and patted her closed mouth like a naughty child.

They'd lived outside, near the tracks, and had eaten "from the hamburger place or cooked out." "Summer living," Queenie called it, and "I never made a kid hunt cigarettes for me. I did my own hunting."

"Did I sleep on a pile of smelly rags?"

"Rags? You had blankets. Everybody brought you things—clothes, toys. The whole yard was looking after you. Don't you remember?"

"What yard?" Carlos asked, and Queenie had laughed.

"The railroad workers. At the station."

"Why were they looking after her?"

"She knows why," Queenie said, gazing at Joelle with solemn eyes.

"Do you know?" Carlos said.

Joelle had shaken her head.

To listen to Queenie was to realize that the old woman had not been some lone crackpot taking advantage of an abandoned child, as Aunt Mary Louise had described her. There was an order to the way she lived then, just as there was now. She'd cared for Joelle, along with others, apparently, and had watched over her, even after Joelle was adopted and moved in with her new family.

"What did Queenie keep thinking you remembered?" Carlos had asked her as they'd walked home. "It had to do with the Crying Rocks."

"Nothing. She was confused, I think."

"She didn't look confused. She knows something else about you. And who is—"

"Don't talk about that!" Joelle had rushed to stop him.

"You don't want to find out?"

"I don't know."

"Why not? It's so strange."

"Maybe I already know enough," she'd replied, and then, feeling the pinch of invaded territory: "Anyway, what do you care? It has nothing to do with you!"

"That's a good question," Carlos had said. "Why *do* I care? And here's another one. Why did you call me up tonight?"

He'd stood facing her on the dark street while Joelle cast around for a mean reply. But none would come to her, for some reason, and in the end, he'd walked away without saying good-bye.

Now, as she drifts closer to sleep, Joelle puts Carlos and his question in a well-guarded place in her mind where she can consider them later. She thinks back once more to Queenie's campfire, hardly daring to look again at the most important artifact that's risen up out of the Marshfield town park that night, the one she'd felt a need to protect from even Carlos's friendly gaze.

"Sylvie."

She whispers her mother's name once, in the dark. It's enough for now.

———————

They are expecting visitors. This is what Vernon tells Joelle when she appears downstairs late the next morning, still in her nightgown.

"When?"

"Now. Soon. I don't know," Vernon says. "Go get dressed."

He's jumpy and mysterious and has already been out to the store to buy supplies: beer, soda, chips, some sliced cold cuts, and bread.

"Are they coming for lunch?" Joelle asks in disbelief. They've never had anyone for lunch. The only people she can think of who would barge in like this on a Sunday morning are Aunt Mary Louise's Tiverton relatives, but they've written her off now, once and for all. Aunt Mary Louise's ashes are buried here, on this side of Narragansett Bay, not in Tiverton with them.

"If they want lunch, they can have it," Vernon declares.

The next thing Joelle knows, he's carrying out a pile of newspapers that's been accumulating in a corner by the front door for about four months—ever since Aunt Mary Louise died. Then he's getting out the vacuum and running it over the living-room rug and onto the bare linoleum of the kitchen. He pushes the TV back against the wall and brings down a couple of chairs from upstairs.

"How on earth many are coming?" Joelle demands, which makes Vernon stop and look at her.

"Everybody," he answers. "They'll all be here. You're going to get an earful, so go up and dress."

When she stands there, not moving, her arms folded stubbornly across her chest, he says: "Scoot! This is a big day in your life, you just don't know it yet. You might not want to live here anymore when this day is over."

"What is that supposed to mean?"

"Just what it says."

"Well, I have something to ask you about first."

"Not now," Vernon tells her.

"It's about Queenie."

"Who?"

"You know, the lady who lives in the park and drives around in that red Bug."

"Oh, Queenie," Vernon says. "I guess she finally got ahold of you."

"Last night, and she said—"

"I can bet I know what she said," Vernon cuts in. "What she's been waiting to sneak up and say for years. Why she had to come around here, I don't know. She didn't want to let go of you and followed us over from New London. At least she left Mary Louise alone, and she better! I told her I'd put the cops on her if she came near us. That's the only way to get through to her, scare the daylights out of her."

"What are you talking about?" Joelle shouts. "I can't understand one thing you're saying!"

"Well, don't worry, you will," Vernon replies. At that moment they hear the sound of wheels turning into the driveway. A car door slams shut, and feet start walking up the steps of the porch.

"Go on, get!" Vernon says, pushing her toward the stairs. "Put on a clean shirt and brush that hair. You want to look like something to them."

"Why?" Joelle says, stubborn as she can be.

"You know why."

"No, I don't."

"Queenie told you."

"Well, you tell me. I want to hear it from you."

Vernon gazes at her a second longer than usual. Then he heaves a kind of desperate

218

sigh, as if he's throwing in the towel at last.

"Because they're your people coming to see you, Joelle. You said you don't want secrets, and I'm taking it serious. Now go on. I've got to let them in the door."

She runs up the stairs and tries to see out the window to the driveway, but the porch roof is in the way, so she races into her room to get dressed. By the time she comes out, a chorus of men's voices is coming up out of the living room: "Hello." "How ya doing?" "Nice place." "Where's the chick house?" "I took the highway." "Well, I came up Route 2 and crossed on 138."

Then another car arrives, more guys come in, and the racket rises another notch. Into this boil of conversation Joelle descends, as nervous as she's ever been about entering a room. For a few moments nobody notices her standing by the stairs, and she gets a good look at the company. They are who she thought they would be, the tall, dark men she saw crowding around Vernon at the funeral. They're not in suits anymore. They have on casual clothes that anyone would wear on a Sunday—Levi's, T-shirts, jogging sneakers. One has boots like Vernon's. That they're all related is easy to see, not only because of their black hair and eyes. It's the way they're carrying on together—breezy, joking, not afraid to touch.

"Come on over here, Joelle," Vernon calls out when he notices her. Before she can even breathe, they've turned around and are grinning at her. One of them does a big, fake double take as if he's never seen her before, and says: "Whoo-eee! How you've grown! Who would've thought that sad little sprout we knew back then would've come out like this?"

"She's not done yet, from what I hear," says another.

"She's got Sylvie in her. Look at that pretty complexion," another declares.

Then, just when Joelle's starting to feel her face flame up, a terrible silence descends and no one can think of how to go on. It seems they've been putting on a brave show for her. They're not so sure of themselves after all. Joelle folds her arms across her chest and stares them down.

Vernon clears his throat. "I guess we all know why we're getting together today," he blurts out.

"I guess so," somebody murmurs. Others nod, a little sadly now, or thoughtfully. And this is the place where Joelle decides to wade in. Loud and clear, she says:

"Well, *I* don't know! So are you going to fill me in or what?"

Everybody laughs, except Vernon, who looks as if he'd like to make a swift escape.

"I guess I'm the one who should start," he tells Joelle, "because I'm the one that caused Sylvie to have to run off to Chicago. If I hadn't've done what I did, she would've stayed right down there at Charlestown and learned to live a quiet life."

"Well, she never would've done that!" one of the men breaks in.

"Sylvie was not destined for a quiet life," another says. "Do you remember how she hitchhiked up to Providence that time . . ."

". . . and took a job at a coffeehouse where folks read poetry at night. . . . This was way before you came on the scene, Vern," a third puts in.

"At fourteen! She was serving drinks and all. How'd she get hired at that age?"

"She was tall, that's how." (They're all weighing in now.)

"She was writing poetry herself! Spirit poems, she called them. She was into her heritage. I went up and saw her."

"Sylvie was writing poetry on top of everything else?"

"And reading it to the college kids up there."

"Who'd that girl think she was?"

"Royalty, that's who. Ready to lead a nation. She took that old Indian story Ma told us seriously."

"I heard people say she wasn't that bad. At poetry, I mean."

"Until they found out how old she really was, I'll bet."

"I was in Chicago then, working my first yard job. What happened?"

"Well, the public school caught up with her that time . . ."

"And she pulls out her little pocketknife . . ."

"She was a wildcat."

"She'd never hurt anybody, though."

"The school, you say?"

"She was dragged home again, for the tenth time. Ma was having a fit!"

It's in this way, with everybody jumping on board and cutting each other off and disputing the facts, that Joelle finally meets her mother, Sylvie, and Sylvie's older brothers, her uncles. All five of them are there in her living room. Not that anybody takes time to introduce himself. Only by listening does Joelle begin to understand: They've been nearby the whole time, knowing her, watching her, knowing her mother, and not saying a word to her about it.

"But why . . . ?" she tries to ask, and her question gets drowned out.

Jodie and Jerry, the twins, are oldest and the only ones who still work for the railroad—where they all worked, with Vernon, at one time, it seems. Then comes Roger, the tallest at about six three, who's now at the turkey farm with Vernon. After him is Frank, in the Rhode Island Highway Department. Everyone calls him Franko. And finally, Greg, wearing his hair long and braided like an old-time Indian because, it turns out, he's a guide at the Pequot Museum over in Connecticut, knows his history inside and out.

"He used to look normal," Uncle Jodie says, rolling his eyes at Joelle, "when he worked in the freight yard up in Worcester. That was around the time you came through on the CSX line, and we had to transfer you over for New London."

"Me?" says Joelle.

"Sure, don't you remember your ride across the country?" Uncle Greg asks.

"Well, I—"

"Eating peanut butter and jelly sandwiches the whole way from a brown paper bag? You didn't half get through them. The leftovers were stiff as a board by the time you hit Worcester."

"I think I—"

"And a couple of screw-top jars full of water. Jerry met you in Cleveland—he was the yard conductor there—and climbed on till Buffalo. Then Jodie came on and brought you down to meet me in Worcester. He was in shipping, like Franko here. They had you fixed up in a special car that was carrying new parts for a nuclear sub down in New London. Good suspension, remember that, Jodie?"

"Sure do. Better than the paying passengers were getting coming in on the New England Central. You got a fast ride, too, because New London was in a hurry to take delivery for its sub."

"But—"

"You were five years old," Uncle Greg says. "Never cried a single drop. A real trooper after all you'd been through."

"What—"

"Can't you remember anything? That's how you came from Chicago!"

15

NOT UNTIL AFTERNOON DOES JOELLE start to discern the amazing scope of her story, which has lain just over the horizon all this time, waiting to be discovered. The way it comes at her in bits and pieces, she has to fight to put everything together.

To begin with, Vernon never does tell what he did. Joelle sees it in his face, though: He was caught by love. One night, two nights, however many it was, Sylvie came away with something from him she didn't want. Her big brother Roger had brought Vernon home from the station at Westerly for dinner one evening, and that was that. They fell for each other.

"We don't blame Vernon," Uncle Greg says.

"If you could've seen Sylvie in those days,

she was one fast item," Uncle Jerry concurs. "Mad at the world for who she was and who she wasn't. Nobody was telling her what to do."

"Vern was the one needed protection," Uncle Jodie declares.

"Where was Aunt Mary Louise?" Joelle asks.

"At the chicken-packaging plant," Vernon answers glumly. "We were just meeting up. No, that's not true, we were together." He lowers his head in shame. "Not married yet, but together, the same as being married. I lost my head with Sylvie. For about one week, that's all it took."

"So then what?"

Then, Vernon recounts, Sylvie went off, not telling anybody anything. Disappeared. She was twenty-two by then, long out of high school, working in an office and perfectly capable of taking care of herself. For a while she was just gone, and nobody heard from her at all. Then a note came from Chicago saying that she'd landed there.

"A few months later comes another postcard announcing that she's had a baby," Franko says, shaking his head. "Ma could've died. She said, 'Now my girl's started making a mess of her life. She's not even married!' Of course, what we didn't know then was that the family tradition had got carried on and she'd had twins."

"Twins!" Joelle says. "Well, that wasn't me."

Franko looks at her.

"So Ma decides to go and visit her," Roger continues. "I was living at home still, commuting up to the Providence station for yard work. That's when you and Jodie and me started going to the ball games in Pawtucket, remember, Vern?"

Sitting beside him, Vernon nods. "Roger and me were pals from way back, in school," he tells Joelle. "He helped me get my first job on the railroad."

"Just like Vern helped me land the turkey-ranch job I've got now," Roger says. "Anybody who tried to pull the old 'Where's your tomahawk, Squanto?' stuff, Vern would knock his block off. He never prejudged anybody, back then the same as now."

The living room has emptied out a bit. Uncles Greg and Jerry have taken a break. They're out looking at the chicks. This story has been going on all through the cold cuts and sodas of a late lunch and now is into midafternoon, when people have got to get out and stretch.

"Anyway, I had Ma all set up with a discount first-class sleeper ticket that would've taken her down to New York and then to Chicago," Roger goes on. "I was proud of handing her that ticket. But at the last minute she gets sick and can't go."

"That was the start of her heart troubles," Uncle Franko says.

"And then nobody goes," Vernon says with a groan. "If somebody had just gone out there, we might've known what was what."

"It's not as if Sylvie asked for company," Roger says. "She knew whose those babies were. She could've asked for help if she needed it."

"I should've gone," Vernon moans. "I let her go, is what I did. I just never even thought . . ."

"He just never even thought those babies were his!" Roger turns to tell Joelle. "We didn't know either, not even Ma. See, Sylvie was a proud one. She didn't want to be caught pregnant by somebody she hadn't planned on, especially someone who's, you know . . ." Roger looks over apologetically at Vern.

"White," Vernon supplies.

"Might as well say it," Vernon declares. "I wasn't up to her standards."

They all fall silent for a minute to delicately acknowledge this truth. From outside in the yard, Joelle hears voices, laughter. The shed contingent is making its way back from viewing the chicks.

"Anyway, three years go by . . . ," Jodie starts up again.

"I finally persuade your Aunt Mary Louise to marry me," Vernon tells Joelle.

"Yeah. From Sylvie, we get telephone calls, a couple of letters," Roger says. "We find out she's got two babies up there, not just one. Ma thinks Sylvie's thinking of going to college, or maybe even *is* going; but, of course, Sylvie being Sylvie, we don't know for sure. She never wanted to let anyone in on her business. It would've been like her to try to pull off a stunt like that. Go to a fancy, white college with a couple of babies on her hands, and working, and by herself."

"You think she was by herself? A girl who

looked like that?" Jerry asks. He's just coming in through the kitchen with Greg.

"She would if she was smart," Franko says. "She had enough babies to take care of without some big lug hanging around. No offense, Vern."

Vern flashes an all clear with his hand.

"And smart is one thing you've got to give her," Franko goes on. "Did you know," he adds, turning to Joelle on the couch, "that Sylvie was ranked number one at her high school? Head of the class her graduating year. An Indian girl. Made people sit up and take note, I can tell you."

"And that was after she'd been absent for most of the whole year before, when she took off and went down to Florida with Queenie," Jerry says.

"What?" exclaims Joelle. "What did Queenie have to do with Sylvie?"

"Queenie's her aunt," Franko says.

"Your great-aunt," Jodie adds.

"Well, our aunt too," Jerry has to admit. He's just drawn up a chair. "She's Ma's crazy sister who came up from Barbados thirty years ago. And never recovered, I guess. Kings and queens on the brain. That's why they call her that. Her real name is Florence."

"She's got a grand sense of herself, all right," Franko says. "I'm beginning to think it runs in the women of this family. I hope you didn't catch it," he adds, winking at Joelle.

"Well, as to kings and queens, even Ma did say—," Roger begins.

"Hush up with that nonsense," Jerry cuts in. He glances at Joelle. "Don't put it in her head. We're no more related to the royal Narragansetts than the queen of England. It's been three centuries, folks."

To Joelle, he says: "Ma grew up down there in Barbados. The way the story is, her family's the offspring of Native Americans who were sold out of Boston after losing to the English in the seventeenth century. When Ma came here to Rhode Island as a kid, she met up with our dad, who's got Indian heritage from way back."

"Or had it," Franko says. "He's been dead awhile. He was proud of his blood. And he was a good railroad man. Showed us the way."

All five brothers sit quietly for a minute, gazing into one another's faces and remembering their father.

"Well, what happened next?" Joelle asks impatiently. "Did you ever find out if Sylvie got through college in Chicago? There's another thing, too—when did I get born?"

Now there's a big silence, a different kind from the first embarrassed one that morning when they were all just meeting and no one knew what to say. This is a silence, Joelle detects, made out of everyone knowing exactly what to say and no one wanting to say it.

Greg is sitting closest to Joelle on the couch. He reaches over and touches her softly on the arm.

"You've *been* born, Joelle. Didn't you understand that?"

"How could I have been born?" Joelle replies. "So far, she's just had Vernon's twins. What were they, by the way, girls or boys? You haven't said yet."

Vernon takes a swallow of the Coke he's drinking.

"Girls," he says, gazing at the carpet. All the uncles keep quiet.

"Well, what were their names?"

"She called one Sylvia, after her, and the other was Sissie. I never knew the names until later, you understand, after the accident." Vernon sounds weak, as if he's run out of breathing power.

Joelle is about to yell *What accident?* when her mind does a little loop around Sylvia and Sissie, and she stops. She knows who they are. They are her being born, right there in front of her eyes.

"I'm already here, aren't I?" she asks Uncle Jerry, sitting across from her, just to make sure.

He nods.

"Well, which one am I?"

"Sissie," he says. "Sylvia was the second one, born too small."

"What does that mean?"

"It means she's got things missing," Vernon jumps in to say. "So she's slow. She's the slow one who wouldn't grow. We only found this out later."

Uncle Jodie is nodding. "Now we know what our sister Sylvie was up against. Not only trying to make her way on an uphill road she's determined to take, stubborn as she is, not only dealing with two little children all by herself, but one of them is retarded. With physical handicaps we don't even know. Not only that, the child gets sick as she gets older. This little girl begins to get real sick."

"And Sylvie doesn't want to leave her with strangers," Uncle Franko says. "You can guess she wouldn't want that, being who she is."

"Sylvie was in trouble," Uncle Jerry says with a nod. "We know that now, thinking back to what she wrote in her letters."

"The problem was, we weren't paying attention," Uncle Jodie says. "Ma was ailing and . . ."

"And then Ma dies," Uncle Roger takes over, with a sigh. "I was still living with her. Vern and I had moved over to working on the turkey ranch. So Sylvie comes home for the funeral, bringing you and Sylvia, age about what? Three?" He looks around at the others for confirmation.

"Four," says Vernon. "I saw my babies. I'd been doing some addition and . . ."

"We still didn't know they were Vern's, did we?" Roger says, looking around at his brothers. They shake their heads.

"I knew," Vernon said. "When I saw them, there wasn't any doubt in my mind. I didn't go up to Sylvie, though. Mary Louise was with me at the service." He gazes across at Joelle, his eyes turning red and watery. "I looked at you . . . and little Sylvia . . . from a distance," he says.

When Joelle sees his eyes, she feels a prickle come up behind her eyes too, because she's just figured out something else. Something she hadn't ever thought possible before.

"You're my father, aren't you?" she says to Vernon.

He nods.

"And Aunt Mary Louise never did know it."

Vernon shakes his head.

"Well, couldn't you at least have told me?" Joelle asks.

Vernon wipes his eyes like a little child. "I couldn't. You would've told her."

"I guess I would," Joelle has to say. "But would it have been so bad if she knew?"

"I didn't know what she'd do. I knew it would hurt her. What if she wanted to leave? I couldn't've stood that. I loved her. She was my good luck."

Vernon puts his big hands over his big face and just moans in what sounds to Joelle like pure agony. "I was caught," he says, muffled behind his hands. "I didn't know which way to go. So I kept quiet."

"And we helped him," Uncle Roger says, standing up tall. "Don't blame him, Joelle. You can't blame anybody. It's the mess things got into."

For a minute Joelle sits where she is, thinking about this. Everybody's eyes are on her, and she's trying to get her bearings. Finally, just as Uncle Roger decides to sit down again and Vernon is accepting a tissue from Uncle Jodie's pocket, she gets them. She stands up.

"That certainly takes care of everything," she says, all five feet nine inches of her looking down on her uncles. "Everything except me and Aunt Mary Louise. I see how it is. Now that she's died, you all can come out of hiding. That's why you're here—isn't it?— because she can't be. Well, I think it's rotten," Joelle says, her voice rising. "I know Aunt Mary Louise would think so too. You went around behind her back. You waited until—"

"That's not true, Joelle," Uncle Jerry protests. "None of us could've known your dear aunt was going to leave us when she did."

"Mary Louise was a star, we all say so," Uncle Greg adds, nodding. "She was batting one thousand in our book. She loved Vern and brought you up good and always kept her head when the going got tough. I think she might even have guessed something wasn't right, and kept her mouth shut."

Joelle doesn't buy it. She thinks she sees the whole story now. If this really were baseball, she'd be in the ninth inning, with the last batter up and a big, lopsided score against her.

"Get out of this house," she's suddenly yelling at the top of her lungs. "Now!" she yells. "This is Aunt Mary Louise's house. She still lives here. You can't get rid of her that easy. Go on, all of you. Get out!"

———————

There's a long silence in the room. Finally, the uncles get up off their chairs, heads hanging, and go outside to the backyard, followed by Vernon.

"C'mon to the shed and let her cool off," Joelle hears him say. They all lumber across the muddy yard—she's watching their every move from the kitchen window—and disappear inside with the chicks, which are just in the process of hatching out for Vernon's next big delivery. With all this coming and going from the shed, it's pretty obvious to Joelle now who his secret backers are!

Joelle gets a can of Coke from the fridge, walks out to the front porch, and strides up and down a few times, venting into the chilly 5:00 P.M. air. It might be spring, but winter's not letting go. Farther north, Chicago's even colder, she's heard. Icy winds off Lake Michigan. Snow in the streets. The biggest drifts last through April some years.

Looking down one of those canyons of Chicago skyscrapers she's seen on TV, Joelle catches a glimpse of Sylvie with her twins, Sylvia and Sissie, crossing a busy street. Sylvie, instructing her girls to look both ways, holding their hands hard—too hard!—while the traffic roars by. There is Sylvie's long black hair rippled by the wind, streaked across her dark face as they turn into the park. Now she is showing her daughters how to make an Indian trail in the snow, as their ancestors did. Put your foot exactly into the footprint of the person in front of you, she explains. In this way, you can hide and fool your enemy. Many can travel under cover of one.

Armed with the uncles' new facts, Joelle believes she remembers this actual scene. She gazes across the divide of years and watches as her footprints tuck neatly inside her mother's big ones. Behind her comes her sister Sylvia, stumbling and breathing hard but doing her best. All this city and traffic and snow are too much for her. Her scared eyes look up and:

"Don't worry, Sylvia, I'll take care of you," Sissie tells her. "Follow me. You can do it."

And she does! Her little foot comes down exactly in the middle of Mom's and Sissie's prints and immediately gets lost. Good work, Sylvia! No one would ever know she was there.

16

JOELLE IS STILL OUT ON THE PORCH, beginning to feel the cold and wondering what her next move will be, when she sees a shadow depart from the sidewalk across the street and come toward her. She recognizes it at once.

"Tonto!"

"*Buenas tardes.*" He approaches carefully through the prickly hedge. "I thought I'd just come by for a minute and . . . find out how you are," he ends lamely.

"I'm alive, as you see." She wants to smile but finds herself frowning. Her guard has gone up. It's obvious he didn't "just come by." He's been out there on the street lying in wait, spying on her, hardly better than the Secret Princesses. She can't stand being tracked that way.

"How did you know where I lived?" she demands.

Carlos shrugs. He looks at her, not angrily as she deserves. His patience always surprises her.

"Look, I'm in the middle of something," she says more kindly. "It's not a good time."

"I saw all the cars in your driveway. I guess you have company."

"I guess I do."

"Okay," he says, and turns to go, but some awkwardness in the way he moves, a peculiar angle of his head, sends Joelle a message. She knows him well enough to read him. Something has happened.

"Carlos, wait. What is it?"

He looks back with reluctance, not eager to be shot down again.

"I'm sorry," she says. "I'm having a crazy day."

"Me too," he admits. "I've been getting some things straight with my father. Last night when I came back from the park, I couldn't sleep. He was awake too, and we started talking."

The park. To Joelle, it seems an age ago. She has to struggle to get on his wavelength. "Did you talk about Daniel?"

Carlos nods. "It was being with Queenie last night. I kept thinking about the Crying Rocks."

"Did you tell your dad that you remembered . . . ?"

"I told him," Carlos says. He takes a deep breath. "Joelle, he said it couldn't have happened that way."

"What do you mean?"

"What I heard couldn't have been Daniel. He was hurt too bad."

"How does he know?"

"He said Daniel's jaw was broken. He couldn't have opened his mouth to make a noise like that. He couldn't even speak. It puzzled my dad later, wondering what I could have heard. He never brought it up, though. He didn't want to remind me of the accident. He was hoping I could forget."

"Well, you almost did."

"He never blamed me, either," Carlos says, sounding as if he can't believe it. "In fact, the opposite; he said I'd been brave. When he was carrying Daniel out, he said I hung in and was tough."

"I'm glad you talked," Joelle says. "You must feel a lot better."

Carlos nods.

"What does he think you heard?"

"He didn't say. I was a little kid. He probably believes I imagined everthing."

"Did you?"

"Well, did I?" Carlos asks her straight back. "You were there, you heard those cries. Did you imagine them?"

"No. And they had nothing to do with the wind."

"So what were they?"

They stand silent on the porch, looking out at the darkening street. Into Joelle's mind comes that hulking mass of glacial boulders, and the swamp beside them, and the forest behind. She hears Queenie's voice say again:

"A ghost is a ghost. It can do what it wants."

She turns toward Carlos. "Relatives of mine have come to visit."

"I saw them out in the backyard. They're

the guys from the funeral, aren't they? The ones who look like you?"

"Right." Joelle glances at him. "You didn't say they looked like me before."

"You would've been mad. You don't like people telling you things like that, remember?"

"They're Native American. Did you know that?"

"I might have," Carlos says. He's being extra careful.

"They've been filling me in on some things."

"I won't ask what," Carlos says, moving away. "I know it's your business." He walks fast toward the sidewalk.

"Wait," Joelle calls, "I want to tell you about Vernon. Do you have to leave now?"

"I have to," he answers over his shoulder. He's been burnt once too often. She can see he doesn't want to risk it again.

"But I'm not sure what I should do."

"You'll figure it out."

"Maybe I'll see you tomorrow?"

"Maybe." He doesn't look around.

"Thanks for coming over!" Joelle shouts after him. This time there's no answer. She watches as the dark outline of his departing body blurs into the street shadows and disappears.

———————

When the uncles return from the chick shed a half hour later, knocking cautiously on the back door, Joelle is waiting for them in the living room with the lamps turned on. The sun has gone down. Outside it's that blue gray dark of early evening, and Carlos was right—she's figured things out. There are a number of matters that have yet to be addressed. Joelle intends to shed light on all of them. First and foremost:

"Where is my sister Sylvia?"

The uncles are coming through the kitchen, grabbing up handfuls of pretzels from the bowl on the counter, when she puts this question to them.

"Now, Joelle. Don't be rushing things," Uncle Jerry says. "We were thinking of going out for a bite, down to the Red Dragon. Do you like Chinese? We'd be honored to escort our niece to dinner."

This, Joelle suspects, is another trick. The uncles have been plotting how to get around her out in the shed. It's laughable to think the only ploy they could come up with was food.

"I am not that dim," Joelle tells them. "Neither am I forgiving you for one thing. The only reason I'm letting you back in this house is that I need some answers. So, if we're going to have Chinese, somebody better go get it. And by the way, don't you all have families waiting for you somewhere? Did somebody invite you to spend the night?"

"Joelle, honey," says Uncle Greg, "you don't have any idea of what happens when us boys get reunited."

"About once in a blue moon since Ma died," Uncle Jodie says, shaking his head.

"Well, what happens," Uncle Greg goes on, "is that we stay and powwow a good long time, till we feel back together again. For myself, I took off from the Pequot Museum till Tuesday. How about all of you?"

"I'm good through tomorrow," Uncle Jerry says. "And for your information, I've got three boys and a girl over in Pawcatuck, all cousins of yours," he adds to Joelle.

"I'm out of the yard till Wednesday," Uncle Jodie chimes in. "Live up in Pittsfield, Mass., these days. Two kids in Connecticut with their ma."

"Well, Vern and I signed out from the turkey ranch for all of this week," says Roger. "Now that Vern's back to being single like me, we're thinking to take a little trip over to view the Paw Sox's opening games. Just a couple of nights, Joelle. Nothing to worry about."

Uncle Franko's not so organized. He says he'll have to call in sick to the R.I. Highway Department. Oh, yes, and he's married with five.

While this summation is under way, Vernon goes in search of his wallet and heads off to the Red Dragon to get the food.

"There's another question I have," Joelle says as they wait. "Why did I need to ride a freight train from Chicago?" She turns to Uncle Roger. "Here you get your mother a first-class sleeping ticket, and you can't even put me in a passenger car?"

"Good question," Roger says. "I'll shoot that over to Jerry. He set it up."

"We had to get you out fast, is the answer,"

Uncle Jerry says, shrugging. "We were one step ahead of the law."

"You're kidding," Joelle says.

"I am not. You had foster care on your tail. Once you disappear into that system, it takes wild horses to get you out. See, by then, we saw how Vern wasn't going to run interference to get you back after the accident. Even though he cared, he was too scared of losing his Mary Louise. So we all pitched in to take action."

Uncle Roger nods. "We wanted you. You were part of our Sylvie, crazy as she was."

Joelle looks away fast. There's something about the way Roger has said this that, combined with the word "accident," frightens her.

"The trouble was," Uncle Frank continues, "we didn't have good standing to take you in custody without some proof. It would've cost us time and money to convince people out there of what was what, if we ever could. So . . ."

"We stole you," Uncle Jerry declares. "Snuck you out of the holding bin where they'd stashed you, put you on the freight and rode you out of there. I had friends in a couple of convenient places from when I worked in Chicago those two years. We got you on board and that was that. The authorities never hardly blinked."

"They let a little child just disappear?" Joelle says, shocked.

"Oh, honey, the way things were back then, they could've lost a truckload without too much trouble. You know, foster kids aren't a high priority to the state politicians. They can't vote yet."

"But I still don't understand. What happened to my mother? And where was Sylvia?"

The next second the front door flies open, and there is Vernon, arms piled high with Styrofoam containers. Everybody jumps up to help carry them into the kitchen.

"Looks like Vern got enough to feed a Continental army," Uncle Franko declares.

"It'll boil down," Vernon replies, and everybody laughs.

"That's for sure," Uncle Greg snorts. "Over at the Pequot Museum we cart out a ton of trash a day, just from lunch and dinner."

"This country's sinking under a mountain of rubbish, and they call it progress," Uncle Franko says, shaking his head. "I'd just like to know what and where they think they're progressing to."

In the midst of this chatter, Joelle is working away on trying to solve the mystery of Sylvie and Sylvia. She plugs the word "accident" into her equation of known facts and comes up with an image. It's a high-rise city apartment building. Porches stacked up the side, one on top of the other. Third floor.

Uncle Roger, settling down next to her with a full plate of food, hears the result.

"My sister fell, didn't she?" Joelle tells him.

Uncle Roger stops moving. He sits absolutely still, not looking at her.

"It wasn't me who fell, was it? The story got mixed up. It was her."

"It was her, not you."

"And she didn't make it."

"No, she didn't," Roger says, a little catch in his voice.

Joelle nods. "I always wondered—how I could've lived through that fall with not even one scar to show for it. I used to look all over my body, and I never found any. Now I know why."

She stares around the room. A tightness is

rising in her chest. She dreads the next question, but she has to ask it.

"Sylvia wasn't thrown, was she? That's the story that came down, but I never believed it."

The chitchat has stopped. Uncle Jerry and Uncle Jodie are standing in the kitchen doorway gazing at Joelle while Uncles Greg, Roger, and Franko are sitting stiff as boards, their plates on their knees. Joelle guesses they were hoping to put this off until after supper.

"Did Sylvia get thrown, or didn't she?" Joelle demands.

Vernon says softly, "She didn't. They went down together."

Joelle looks straight ahead. She takes a little sip of air and turns to Roger, sitting beside her.

"You mean, somebody else went too?" she asks, and Roger cannot answer. He glances across at Vernon for help.

"Joelle, there was no somebody else," Vernon says. "Sylvie would never take her kids to somebody else, that was the problem."

"So who went down?" Joelle says, even though she knows the answer. It's right in front of her, clear as day, like the answers on the tests at school that never give her any trouble.

"My mother?" she says. "Sylvie took my sister down?"

Vernon puts his plate on the floor with a clatter and leans toward her.

"Joelle, this is what we found out, after. In the end, Sylvie wasn't bringing little Sylvia to the doctors anymore. She saw there wasn't anything they could do. But even more, what we think now is, she didn't want to leave her girl in the hospital. Sylvia was real weak. Her heart was bad and she couldn't breathe right. She had been in the hospital a lot of times before and she hated it. She was terrified of the hospital. Your mother was determined to keep her home."

"She telephoned me a couple of days before," Roger breaks in.

"Who?" Joelle asks him.

"Your mother. She'd call me every once in a while, probably out of habit from before Ma died. I was still living at the old house. This time, Sylvie told me things were going downhill fast with Sylvia and she wasn't going to stop them. Sylvia had suffered enough. She asked me: Was there any way I could come out and take care of Sissie for a spell? She didn't want you there, Joelle, when the end came. So I said, yes, I'd take some time off. And I was on my way. God knows, I was on the road, driving out there, when . . ."

Vernon clears his throat loudly, and speaks. "He would've been there the next night, as you all know," he tells the room at large. "Roger was coming. Sylvie knew he was coming. Now, Joelle, this is what happened.

"A social worker came by Sylvie's apartment to check up on how things were, and she saw little Sylvia and ran off to get help. And Sylvie wouldn't let her back in the door, so this social worker called Emergency. Then the medics came and Sylvie wouldn't let them in either. When they tried to break in anyway—"

"My mother made me stay in the bedroom," Joelle says. Her voice surprises her. It sounds high and squeaky like a child's.

"You remember this?" Vernon looks at her hard.

"I'm just now remembering some things."

"Well, you were there, of course. Nobody was going to ask you what happened. You were too little."

"She said I had to stay. I didn't want to. It wasn't my fault."

"Your fault?" asks Uncle Roger, but Joelle hardly hears him.

Inside her mind she's gazing far off to another time, to a place so well forgotten it was all but erased. It's a room with a window that looks out over an open-air porch.

"She told me she was going out the window, onto the porch with Sylvia, because Sylvia had to go away, and she couldn't go alone," Joelle remembers. "Somebody was pounding on the door."

"Well, that was most likely Emergency," Vernon says quietly. The uncles are not eating anything. They've forgotten they have plates on their knees.

"I said, 'I want to come too. I am supposed to take care of her,'" Joelle recalls, "but she wouldn't listen."

She sees the room's four walls now, the big window and the two beds with their green quilted bedspreads. One bed is for Mother. The other is for Sissie and Sylvia, who always sleep together, even when Sylvia is very sick, just as they always do everything together. They have to, so Sylvia won't be afraid and Sissie can keep her safe.

"My mother said she was the only person who could keep Sylvia safe now. I had to stay and wait. I didn't want to. I wanted to go!"

"Your mother wasn't thinking straight," Uncle Roger says. "If she was herself, she never would have left you like that." He shakes his head hard, as if he's trying to shake something out of it.

"She told me not to cry or Sylvia would be scared, and I didn't," Joelle remembers. "I sat there and waited, and I never cried once. Even when they broke down the door, I never cried."

"Well, you are now, honey," Uncle Greg says, and Joelle notices that she is. Without any trouble at all, with no fighting back or holding on, her eyes have filled up and overflowed. The uncles have become a wobbling, shimmering sea of heads and bodies. Then their arms are around her, and everybody is crying together for Sylvie and Sylvia. And for her.

———————

Aunt Mary Louise would have been amazed to see how well her house took in the company that night. Those tiny rooms expanded to fit the Indian uncles with no trouble at all. There could have been even a few more bodies squeezed in—and maybe this will come to pass, Joelle thinks, if any of the dozen or so cousins she's been hearing about decides to pay a visit. Considering that she was running out of space before, filling the place up all by herself, it's a remarkable alteration.

On her way through the living room to the kitchen the next morning, Joelle steps over the snoring forms of the twin uncles, Jerry and Jodie. They're tucked into a couple of sleeping bags, using rolled-up sweatshirts for pillows. Uncle Franko is sprawled on the couch in his underwear, and Uncle Greg's mass of black braid is sticking out from a snarl of blankets beside the dining table.

Uncle Roger is asleep upstairs with Vernon, the last six inches of his six-foot three-inch frame hanging off the bottom end of Aunt Mary Louise's side of the bed. Joelle caught a glimpse going by in the hall, and it gave her a good feeling. She's not sure what Aunt Mary Louise would think, but she likes seeing Uncle Roger there. His tallness is her tallness. Uncle Greg's black tuft of braid looks a lot like her hair when she gets up in the morning. These men knew her mother when she was Joelle's age. They grew up with her in the same house and spoke to her every day. They're sitting on top of an entire world she's going to get to know—and one that's going to get to know her.

She's on her way to school. School of all things! In the middle of all this. It's Monday morning, and unlike Vernon and the uncles—who are not setting a very good example in this regard—she can't call in sick or take time off. Not anymore. A day job you can fudge, but school marches ahead, with or without you. It's up to you to hang in there. One thing Joelle's been sure of for the last few months is that she's going to carry on for Aunt Mary Louise. Now she has Sylvie and

Sylvia to work for too. This morning, as a start, she's planning to ace a Spanish test on irregular verbs. Standing at the kitchen counter, she's eating a bowl of cereal and studying her Spanish textbook when:

"Joelle?"

It's Vernon, unshaved, barefoot, staring at her from the kitchen doorway with red-rimmed eyes.

"What?"

"I just wondered how you're fixed for today."

"If you mean lunch money, I've got it."

"I didn't mean that." Vernon lowers his voice to a whisper. "What I wonder is, how you're doing with—"

"I'm okay," she says quickly. "I might be late getting home this afternoon. I have to talk to someone."

"Who?"

"Just somebody. Will anyone still be here?"

"Roger and Jerry and Jodie, from the look of it. I'll get up a dinner. You're taking it pretty well, then?"

"What do you mean?"

"I thought after you found out . . . well, you might be disgusted or angry or . . ."

Vernon, in his usual roundabout way, is asking her for something. Joelle knows what it is.

"Do you think I should be angry?"

He shrugs. He looks desperate.

"I don't know how I am yet," she answers him truthfully. "It'll take me a while to figure out. I'm still going to live here, though, if that's what you're asking. I don't plan on moving in with any of these guys." She gestures toward the sleepers in the living room. "Did you really believe I would leave?"

"I didn't know." Vernon hangs his head. "I have a lot to apologize for," he mumbles. "I didn't handle things like I should. I wish your Aunt Mary Louise were here to say what she thinks."

Joelle takes in his misery and closes her Spanish book. "I know what she'd think."

Vernon shakes his head.

"I do. She'd say it was okay."

"Really?" Vernon glances up.

Joelle nods. "She wouldn't leave either."

Vernon looks about ready to cry. "How do you know?" he asks.

"Well, that's the biggest mistake you made of all. You should think about it," Joelle tells him. "You could figure it out if you tried."

"I could?"

"Yes."

He looks faintly hopeful, but also on the verge of asking her *How?* when a series of knocks sounds on the front door. From outside, an urgent voice rings out.

"Joelle! Where are you? It's me! We're going to be late!"

"I have to leave; that's my tribe calling," Joelle says with a grin. She puts out her hand and touches his as she goes by, maybe just to help her squeeze past, but maybe not.

"See you tonight," Vernon says when she's half out the door.

"See you," Joelle answers. And that feels good too.

17

WITH THE COMING OF APRIL, AND THEN May, the weather in Marshfield gradually warms. Showers muddy the yards and gardens frequently at first, then give way to days of sunshine. The swallows return and nest. The catbirds shriek and mimic the cries of babies. Trees break into leaf, and Joelle's interest in the Narragansetts revives, along with her interest in Carlos. He's wised up from their early days, and their research sessions in the library now often end as sparring matches.

Joelle, reading out loud (with a slight smirk) from a book titled *Indian New England, 1524–1674*:

> *"The men, for the most part, live idly; they do nothing but hunt and fish. Their*

*wives set their corn and do all the other
work.*

> —FRANCES HIGGINSON, 1629"

"Oh, yeah?" Carlos counters. "Well listen
to this:

> *"Narragansett men shouldered the most
> dangerous and exhausting duties—hunting
> and fishing, making the bows, arrows and
> canoes, and protecting the tribe and family.*
> —*INDIAN NEW ENGLAND BEFORE
> THE PILGRIMS"*

"So? What about this?" Joelle says. She
reads:

> *"It is almost incredible what burdens
> the poor women carry of corn, of fish, of
> beans, of mats, and a child besides.*
> —ROGER WILLIAMS, 1643"

Carlos laughs scornfully and reads from
another source: *"'For all the assertion that the
squaw was overburdened . . . or that her health
was ruined by labor, little direct evidence can be
found. The excellent physical health attributed to*

women of the agricultural tribes is testimony to the contrary.'"

"Wait a minute. How could they possibly know Narragansett women were in such excellent physical health?" Joelle demands. "They were all wiped out, remember?"

"They found graves. It says right here: *'Narragansett burial sites support evidence of powerful women of extraordinary height.'"*

"Well, that doesn't mean they didn't work harder than the men."

"I never said they didn't."

"I'm just making sure you understand. Women were important back then."

"I understand."

"Hunting and fishing were sidelines for the Narragansetts. Their tribes depended on food that was grown, harvested, and stored by women. Women were crucial to survival!"

"They definitely were. And not only that, they still are," Carlos replies, looking up at her with such ardent sincerity that Joelle is left feeling like an entire Spanish armada becalmed in the heat of battle.

They are friends again. And perhaps a little more than friends, as people usually are who have telephoned one another late at night, and heard each others' extraordinary stories, and discovered links between their lives that are invisible to others.

Carlos has asked: "So Queenie knew you were coming to the New London freight depot?"

And Joelle has answered, as if she'd always known it: "Oh, sure. She was part of my uncles' plan. I needed to drop out of sight for a while, and Queenie was the perfect cover. Vernon told Aunt Mary Louise that I was a lost child picked up by the police, but it was all part of the plan. The Family Services Center she always talked about was a fake my uncles arranged. I was the only kid there. Queenie had just driven me up from the New London depot, where we'd been hanging out that summer."

Joelle has asked him: "How are you and your dad getting along? Is he still going on a lot of trips?"

And Carlos has answered: "He's taking *us* on a trip, my mother and me. We're visiting some Sioux historical sites in South Dakota this summer."

In the midst of this new closeness, there remain private zones between them, places that seem to lie beyond the reach of words or explanations. Even knowing what she now does about Sylvie, Joelle can't imagine how her mother did what she did. Sylvie's choice, and the part Joelle played in it, are matters Joelle can't explain to herself yet, and she keeps the frightening room in the high-rise apartment building locked behind its door in her mind.

Somehow, Carlos is aware of this and doesn't trespass. With equal understanding, Joelle stays away from the subject of Daniel's fall. Though Carlos's father has spoken to him, it's not enough. She can tell that Daniel is often on his mind, a shadowy form following silently behind him on hikes through the woods, a figure watching from the edge of the picture.

Like Sylvia.

Joelle recognizes her twin now. She was there the whole time, as close as Joelle's own skin, separated by only a twist of imagination, which shows how close the past can be to the present. Invisible as Sylvia was before, now that Joelle knows what to look for, she sees her everywhere in her life.

"Remember that long-haired cat I told you

about?" she asks Carlos one day, trudging home from school. "The one that came with me from Chicago on the freight train and ate my peanut butter and jelly sandwiches? I've just figured it out: That was my sister, Sylvia."

"It was?"

"Yes. She wasn't going to be left behind."

"Or you weren't going to leave her," Carlos points out.

"Maybe, but remember the feeling I had that I was being tracked through the woods when we hiked to the Crying Rocks?"

"You also had it coming back," Carlos reminds her.

"That was Sylvia too. She was following secretly in my footsteps, just as our mother taught her to do."

Carlos appears doubtful. "So she's somehow around here in spirit form?"

"In a way. She was that little dog who slept with me in my box at the railroad depot."

"This is all in your mind, of course," Carlos says, to reassure himself of her sanity. Or maybe his.

"Queenie wouldn't think so. Ghosts are real to her. That painting in the library . . ."

"Oh, that painting! I never should have

told you about it. You're turning into a dangerously haunted person," Carlos kids her.

"Maybe I am, but Sylvia is there. That's a picture of her, standing with me in the bushes. I'm holding her hand the way I used to in Chicago. We're looking at our village."

"Seriously haunted," Carlos repeats, shaking his head. "It's a bad case of ancestor worship."

"As if someone who's only one-sixteenth Indian would know anything about my ancestors," Joelle says with a smile.

Carlos nods and grins. "You certainly beat me there." A moment later, his face changes.

"Speaking of ghosts," he whispers. He points behind them, up the sidewalk.

Swinging around to look, Joelle catches sight of a bobble of little-girl heads sneaking along behind the hedge.

"If you don't mind, I'm heading back to the *ranchero*," he says. "I don't want to be yelled at. Your royal followers have been getting a little out of control lately. I think you're beginning to lose your charm."

He takes off at top speed leaving Joelle to face her troops. They are back to wearing braids again, and going a step further, are all sporting beaded bands with exotic feathers from various long-winged birds. Whether they talked their mothers into buying these crazy headdresses at a costume store or made them themselves, it's hard to tell. Whatever, enough is enough. This spy operation must come to an end.

"*Buenos días*, Indian princesses!" Joelle calls out determinedly.

A storm of giggles arises from behind the hedge.

"Come forth and show yourselves!" Joelle calls. "I have a proposition."

"A what?" says one princess, sticking her head around the hedge. They all file out with suspicious eyes. This is the first, the very first time Joelle has consented to speak to them. They're gazing at her skeptically, wondering if it's some kind of trick. Over on one side of the pack, Joelle is happy to see Misti. She's worked things out, it seems, and is back with the others.

"I wish to speak of tribal matters," Joelle addresses them formally. "Give me your leader."

"We can't," one of the princesses pipes up.

"Why not?"

"We threw her out!"

"You did?" Joelle glances at Misti. "You never told me! You threw Penny Perrino out of her own club?"

"It wasn't hers anymore. She was too mean," Misti says.

"Penny wasn't even in our grade. All she wanted was to boss us around," another princess explains. "Now we have meetings when *we* feel like it, and nobody gets cut out."

"Well, that's a relief," Joelle says. "Here's what I was thinking. How'd you all like to know a real Indian queen?"

"Oh, come on. An Indian queen is still alive?"

"How can you tell she's really a queen?"

"Because she told me, and I believe her," Joelle informs them solemnly. "Come and meet her, you'll see." She strides off on her long legs toward the park, the whole of her tribe trotting doubtfully behind.

———

Vernon would not approve, but ever since hearing her story from the uncles, Joelle has been visiting Queenie. She finds her in the park in the late afternoons or, spotting Queenie's red Bug parked outside the library, looks for her there. It's more than information she's after. Some old feeling of comfort and safety has lingered from their days at the depot, though Joelle still recalls little from that time. Being with Queenie simply makes her happy.

Often they sit together without saying anything. The old woman is not always prepared to talk. Certain questions anger her and mention of past events introduces strain and confusion. Whether any event is truly past or is merely biding its time, waiting to come round again, is an issue for her. Small pieces of new information have reached Joelle's ear, though, and there is even the occasional jewel.

About Sylvie, Queenie had volunteered: "She is crying for you. Do you know she misses you?"

"How?" Joelle had asked. "Where is she?"

"There." Queenie pointed vaguely behind her. "In the forest. She cries with the others."

"At the Crying Rocks?" Joelle asked.

Queenie had turned away and hidden her face in her hands.

But another time, about the rocks themselves, she had suddenly burst out: "It's a place the earth keeps for us, our people. In ancient times a mother who had to leave her baby brought him there—a child born sick or unfinished or damaged beyond repair. She knew what she must do, but she was sad, so sad. Can you imagine?"

"When you say mothers left their children, what does that mean?" Joelle had asked. "The mother abandoned the child?"

Queenie had grown confused at this. Shaking her head, she'd answered a different question. "No, no, not Sylvie. Sylvie couldn't leave her girl. She wasn't crazy, like they said. She wanted to stay with you, but she had to go with the little one."

"With my sister?"

"Yes. Sylvie was very brave."

"Did you know her well?"

"Yes," Queenie had whispered. "And I hear her cry."

Now, as Joelle approaches the park with her troop of feathered princesses in tow, Queenie's dark shape can be seen in the distance, moving through the trees. She is usually here at this time, gathering wood for her evening campfire. Subject as she often is to confrontation with the local police, she stockpiles supplies in hidden places near the barbecue pit. Only late at night, after the patrols have passed, does she light her blaze to cook, as Joelle knows now, having been out a few times to sit with her.

"Look!" Joelle tells the Secret Princesses, and their eyes widen, for here comes Queenie in her many-layered outfit, wild hair streaming, not at all what they expected, but certainly something to be reckoned with. Tall and wide, she is a force of nature.

"Sit down and wait," Joelle tells her tribe when they reach the old barbecue pit, and they do, removing their headdresses, which have a tiresome way of falling into their eyes. After some hesitation Queenie approaches and sits too. This is her parlor, after all, and she's become used to seeing Joelle at this hour.

For a while there is nervous silence as Queenie eyes her visitors warily. Finally, Misti, unable to contain herself a second longer, raises her voice.

"Are you really an Indian queen?"

Immediately, the old woman relaxes. She gives Misti a wide, tobacco-stained smile and answers, with immense pride.

"I am related to kings and queens. To kings and queens, that is what they say. And to her," she adds. "It was a secret. Did you know?"

When Queenie points, all eyes turn toward Joelle with sparkling new interest.

The forest, when Joelle and Carlos enter it off the busy road, welcomes them with pungent scents of both decay and new growth. Beneath trees bright with June leaves, last fall's castoffs lie in various stages of boggy digestion, already too far gone to be raised by even the strongest wind. The North–South Trail is clear and dry. They pass along it silently, barely disturbing the ongoing beat of life around them.

"Look," Carlos says in a low voice as two red foxes on the hunt pad across the trail a short distance in front of them. A little while later, coming up on the chattering flow of Cowaset Brook, a wiry doglike creature with a yellowish coat bounds away, sneaking one sharp glance over a shoulder.

"That was a coyote," Carlos says. "You didn't use to see them, but now they're moving in from other areas."

"Why?" Joelle asks.

"Too many roads and houses, I guess. They need uninterrupted territory to live."

The Narragansetts had a similar need, Joelle recalls from her reading. Never rooted to a single place, they moved with the seasons, depending on where the best food supplies could be found. Their villages could be dismantled and packed up in a few hours, and they traveled light, carrying the barest minimum of possessions.

Hefting her knapsack on her back, Joelle tries to imagine how it would feel to live with the land this way, bound to nature's rhythms. Bound to its mysteries as well, the uncertainties and anomalies of the spirit universe, whose relation to the human mind is still far from understood, she thinks suddenly. For as they cross the brook and head away, following the trail's incline, she is aware of a disturbing black mass looming up in her mind's eye. She can't see or hear them, but somewhere to the west, from the edge of their disreputable swamp, she feels the Crying Rocks send out a warning.

She and Carlos are hiking to the high council place. It's a pleasant Saturday morning. They've brought sandwiches and bottled water. School will close for the summer in a week, and they have a plan to make a much longer hike with Carlos's father, over several days, up through southern Massachusetts. The walk today is a preliminary expedition to build stamina.

"Do any of your uncles like to hike?" Carlos asks over his shoulder.

"Greg does. He did a survey of original Native American trails in southern New England for the Pequot Museum. He told me he was out there trying to trace the routes along highways roaring with traffic, in fear for his life half the time."

Carlos laughs. "Maybe he'll come with us on our long hike. We're not going on any roads if we can help it."

"I'll ask him. Vernon would like that. He's always worrying about me these days."

"Well, that's a change," Carlos says. "What's up with him?"

"Don't ask me. He says his good luck has moved over from Aunt Mary Louise to me, so he has to keep an eye on me. It's kind of a pain, but . . ." Joelle shades her eyes against a shaft of sun that's broken through the foliage. For a moment she's blinded, and then: "What was that?" she asks Carlos.

"What?"

"I thought I saw people. Over there, through the trees."

They come to a halt and look, but all is quiet and unrevealing. As they listen the forest around them seems to deepen, to spread away into miles and miles of whispering greenery.

"Nothing moving that I can see," Carlos tells her cheerfully. "What did they look like?"

"I'm not sure," Joelle says, though she knows very well what she saw. The warrior hunters are here, watching them from just beyond the border of time. Their tall, dark forms are woven into the shadows of the trees. Their eyes are spangles of light between the leaves. As she and Carlos set off again the hunters turn silently on their own trail and veer away toward their village, a place so well concealed in the folds of the forest that Joelle knows she will never be able to find them. Like the deer and the coyote, they have slipped through the encroaching ring of highways and towns and come here to hide. Only occasionally, on such hikes as this, will her path cross theirs for one flash of a moment.

Ahead of her Carlos looks over his shoulder and slows a bit, so she can catch up.

"Almost there," he says, bringing her back to solid ground.

The trail rises steadily now, and for a few minutes they push on without speaking. From somewhere to their right, the high rasping screech of a bird rings out, answered by a second screech, much closer by. Joelle glances up, but the foliage above them is too dense to see anything.

"Where are the Crying Rocks from here?" she asks.

"About a mile south," Carlos answers between breaths. They are in the final steep climb toward the ledge, both panting. "Nothing to worry about," he adds, knowing what she's thinking. "There's not even any wind blowing today."

And then they are there, at the high council place, stepping out on top of the world. To Joelle, it's a shock all over again, the long sweep of the view across the valley, the blast of sun in their faces. The trees far below form a carpet of light and dark greens. In some places the leaves are late in coming and the brown scalp of the earth shows through. In another area silver spires of dead wood poke up from a dense cover of low-lying vegetation.

Carlos has taken out a pair of binoculars and begun to look around. He points to the silvery section. "You can see where the swamp begins," he says. "I've never been able to tell where it was before. Later on it's hidden by growth."

Joelle nods. While he stands on the brink, peering here and there through the glasses, she keeps herself well back. For one dizzy moment she'd felt the emptiness below drag her forward with its insistent grip. Now she is released and in charge of herself again.

"What can you see?" she asks.

"I'm looking at the edge of the swamp,"

Carlos answers. "Somebody's walking down there."

She follows his gaze and picks out the dead trunks again. Farther to the left, she's just able to make out a gray outcropping of rock, and she is looking at this, wondering if it could possibly be what she thinks it is, when a long, shrill cry echoes across the valley.

Beside her Carlos jerks the binoculars away from his eyes and goes absolutely still. This is no bird. It's a sound they both recognize, though removed now from its stormy context. Into the sunny silence of a June morning comes that wild, pure, grieving shriek again. And once more.

"Let me see," Joelle says. She takes the binoculars, and focusing on the Crying Rocks, since this is certainly what they are, she catches sight of a tiny human figure moving slowly, with a familiar gait, up one side. As she watches, the cry rings out again, piercing and unearthly, an elemental wail of sorrow and loss.

Below, the lone figure has stopped walking and turned a face toward the outcropping above.

"It's Queenie," Joelle breathes to Carlos,

"but I can't tell if . . ." She peers harder into the binoculars. "I can't quite see . . ."

The old woman begins to move upward again. She passes into the shadow of the rocks and, with infuriating finality, disappears from sight. Joelle turns to Carlos.

"I couldn't tell if she was listening or crying."